CHEYENNE MEDICINE

Mark Holden was due in eight weeks at St Louis to lead a wagon train to California. He came upon an attack on the Kremmling to Granby stage, resulting in the stage-driver being wounded. His prompt action saved the stage but led him to listen to the stage-owner's problems. These involved a pushy mining company, crooked law and a scheming, deadly ramrod who had spread fear amongst the citizens of Kremmling. Holden could only spare Kremmling just two weeks of his time, so he had to move fast. Raised Cheyenne style, he leaned on his Cheyenne friends who owed him allegiance.

CHEYNNE MEDICINE

CHEYENNE MEDICINE

by

Hal Jons

The Golden West Large Print Books
Long Preston, North Yorkshire,
BD23 4ND, England.

British Library Cataloguing in Publication Data.

Jons, Hal
 Cheyenne medicine.

 A catalogue record of this book is
 available from the British Library

 ISBN   978-1-84262-894-2 pbk

First published in Great Britain by Robert Hale Ltd.

Copyright © Hal Jons 1983

Cover illustration © Michael Thomas

The moral right of the author has been asserted

Published in Large Print 2014 by arrangement with
Hal Jons, care of Mrs M. Kneller

The Golden West Large Print is an imprint of Library Magna
Books Ltd.

Printed and bound in Great Britain by
T.J. (International) Ltd., Cornwall, PL28 8RW

ONE

Mark Holden pulled his mount to a stop and gazed at the scene unfolded below with quiet satisfaction. In contrast to the steep, twisting descent he had made since daybreak, the run from the edge of the trail to the valley below where the Colorado River glistened in the sunlight, was smooth and gentle. Fifteen miles to his right, and hidden by the cliff-face, would be Kremmling, and about the same distance to his left would be Hot Sulphur Springs. As he remembered, the rough track that carried the stage-coach from Kremmling to Granby ran alongside the Colorado through a run of canyons, and he decided to travel the stage-coach route before crossing the Divide to Idaho Springs and then Denver.

He drew in a deep pull of tobacco smoke and exhaled slowly before talking quietly to the big, ungainly horse standing splayfooted, bearing his weight with ease. 'Idaho Springs is almost in spitting distance, Chief, an' that's halfway. The other half is easy, an' you ought to know, you've done it a few times.'

The horse grunted as though in agreement, when firing broke out from the bottom of the valley, and a stage-coach came into view, travelling towards Kremmling and spewing up dust in clouds. The shotgun rider was firing as fast as he could load, and as the stage swept on, three riders drew closer to the coach, each one sending bullets towards the dust pall.

Holden slipped the packhorse rein from his saddle-cantle and set his mount to the slope. He reached the cover of a boulder beside the trail, with the stage still a hundred or so yards away. As it came alongside and swept past, he had a brief view of a bewhiskered driver with a bloodstained sleeve and a figure in buckskin atop the coach busy ramming shells into a Winchester repeater. A few riders rounded a bend in hot pursuit and he sent three shots in rapid succession, sending two men to the ground, and another hanging grimly to his seat in the saddle whilst clutching at his shoulder. The other riders pulled up, then lying low over the necks of their mounts rode away as Mark sent a couple more bullets close enough to give them a fright.

He watched while the injured rider hung on to turn and ride away, and with the swaying coach still travelling, Holden rode back up the slope to collect his packhorse. By the time he arrived where the animal stood he saw that the stage had come to a stop. Looking backtrail he saw that the fallen riders had been collected, and the horses with their burdens slung over saddles were led out of his view almost as soon as he had them in sight. Remembering the wounded stage-driver, he rode back to the valley floor and headed towards the stage.

Holden approached the stage-coach carefully, keeping his hands in full view. He could see a little group standing around the injured driver; they were all gaily dressed women except the one who heard his approach. She swung around, holding a Winchester in line with his heart. She was dressed in fringed buckskin jacket, Stetson, Levi's and calf-length boots, and her eyes glistened amidst a face plastered with dust.

'Hold it right there, Mister!' she ordered, and Holden reined in.

'Don't get itchy fingers with that gun, Ma'am. Those hombres would have had you cooked if I hadn't horned in.'

'How do I know it was you took a hand?'

'I don't care much what you think, Ma'am, but it so happens I'm a doctor, and when that driver passed me he looked like he needed any help I could give him.'

The girl lowered the Winchester, and Holden slid out of the saddle, and collecting his medical kit from the satchel on the pack-horse, he walked past the girl and made for the group of ladies around the driver. They broke ranks and stared at him approvingly, but his attention was solely for the stubble-chinned oldster who glowered with bad temper at his disability.

'Just my goldarned luck,' the oldster snarled. 'How in heck am I gonna keep the stage-line going now? With old Rube out of action as well.'

Holden had the man's coat sleeves and shirt cut to the shoulder in a moment, and checking on the wound, looked the oldster straight in the eye. 'I don't know about Rube,' he said, 'but you're not going to be handling that team for a few weeks, that's for sure.'

'Mebbe I can handle the pain,' the driver replied.

Holden didn't answer immediately, but set about cleaning off the wound and cauterizing it before fixing pads and bandages. As he worked he was conscious of the dust-covered face of the girl who had challenged him, at his shoulder. 'Yeah, you'll handle the pain sure enough, but if you don't rest that arm until a doctor tells you it's good and ready, you'll have to learn to manage with one.'

'I'll see he rests up, Mister er – er,' the girl said firmly. 'And thanks for fixing him up.' She paused, and white teeth showed up against the dust covering her face as she smiled.

'The name's Mark Holden, Ma'am, and I'm sure glad to be of service.' He paused, his glance taking in the other four women who were looking at him with undisguised interest. 'Just how far does the stage go?'

'To Kremmling, Mister Holden, this is the Kremmling to Granby stage, and the driver is my father, Dave Lomas, who owns the franchise.'

Holden nodded. 'And you ride shotgun? That's mighty dangerous work for a lady.'

She gave him a level look. 'There's no man who'll do the job better, Mister Holden. Those hombres wouldn't have got much closer.'

Holden grinned, transforming the serious set of his face, and his sunburned, handsome features quickened the interest of the women who had long since transferred their attention from the unfortunate Dave Lomas. 'Yeah, I guess you're right. If I was a bit premature taking a hand, then I sure hope you'll forgive me.'

Kate Lomas looked at him sharply, but there was no artifice in his expression, and at length she smiled, which meant she showed two rows of pearly teeth through a cake of dust. 'You've no call to apologise, Mister Holden, or do we call you Doctor Holden? I'm obliged, nobody in their right senses turns away help.'

'Call me anything you like, Ma'am, Doctor, Mister, or better still, Mark.' He paused to allow the girl to make up her mind, then continued. 'Well, let's get things going. I'll take over the driving. Dave, you'd best ride inside, so one of you ladies had better ride up front with me.'

He turned away to get his horses tied to the rear of the stage, leaving four young ladies to make an undignified scrimmage for the seat alongside the driver. A very determined brunette was safely ensconced in the seat, and three hard-faced women were taking their places inside when Mark returned to help Dave aboard. The girl who had watched the others scrabbling for a place beside the young doctor shrugged her shoulders, and gave what assistance she could to settle her father, then she climbed atop the stage to her shotgun station, clasping her Winchester as easily as though it was an extension of her body.

Holden climbed aboard, and taking up the reins, released the brake and set the team off with a shout, totally unconscious of the side-long glances from the pert brunette at his side. The team had too many miles under its belt to become fractious under a new hand-ler so Mark was able to relax in his seat and enjoy the ride.

The brunette edged closer, trying to catch his eye, and when she succeeded Holden smiled at her. The girl was extremely nice-looking and the level quality in her eyes brought sense to her plain speaking. 'You're quite some man, Mister Holden, being a doctor an' all. I guess you're already married?'

Holden's smile widened. 'Nope. There you're wrong, Ma'am. Never considered the prospect. Just ain't had the time to think of any good reasons why I should.'

'My name's Betsy Gray, Mister Holden, and the way I see it a doctor should have a woman right alongside him, to look out for him when he's so allfired set on looking out for other folk.'

'Can't say I'm agreed with that sort of logic, Miss Gray, and anyway, I've been a sort of roving doctor for the last few years, and I aim to carry on the same way until I get the roving out of my system.' He paused while the expression changed on the girl's face. 'Tell me, where're you heading, Betsy Gray?'

'Kremmling,' she replied at once. 'That's where we're all heading. We answered a paper advertisement back in St Louis to come out and get wed to some folk in Kremmling.' She flashed a quick look at him out of dark, brown eyes. 'But the nearer I get to the blamed place the less I like the thought of teaming up with a saloon potman. I guess I'd settle for a well-set-up doctor any day.'

'Might be better for you all if you arrive in Kremmling sort of incognito,' Mark observed thoughtfully. 'Taking potluck is all right for most things, but marriage I guess needs a bit more than a few words printed in a paper. Mind, you'll not be the first, could be your potman will turn out just right, but like I say, a bit of breathing space, with the chance to find out what's what before announcing yourselves would leave you free to head into the sun if things didn't look too promising.'

Betsy Gray gave him a withering look. 'It's not as easy as that, Mister Holden. The men sent money to get us from St Louis, and there's no way they're not going to want their money's worth.'

Mark Holden shook his head as he pondered the situation of the four young ladies. He took another sidelong glance at the girl beside him, and concluded that there wasn't much that would keep her ebullient spirit down for long. He sighed as he commented, 'Well now, Betsy Gray, I guess the deal looked good enough in St Louis; just keep your fingers crossed and keep hoping things turn out.'

She snorted derisively. 'If that potman don't match up to my requirements then he can go heck, and he'll just have to wait until I can earn enough to pay him back for the ride. Kremmling seemed a long way from St Louis, and that was a good place to get away from. I'd worked those steamboats up and down to New Orleans too long for comfort.

I guess I'd stood out against the pesky hustlers, cardsharps and shysters long enough to make another try doubtful, so I took the chance to get away. It's just that all of a sudden St Louis is beginning to look good again.'

Holden threw her another glance just as he guided the leaders around a bend in the trail, and when he looked ahead again, he saw a large boulder had fallen from the cliff wall onto the middle of the trail. He had to check the team and swerve the leaders wide of the boulder to get clearance, sending the stage rocking. Betsy Gray yelped but held on, there were female shrieks from inside the coach and loud expletives from Dave Lomas, then the head of Kate Lomas appeared over the roof-rail.

'Hey Mister!' she shouted. 'If you're gonna let pretty women turn your head, you just wait until you've got your feet on terra firma. When you're driving a stage there's only one way to look, and that's straight ahead. Maybe we'd better change places, because if I was in that seat I wouldn't have your problems.'

Betsy Gray looked up at the dust-covered face and replied cuttingly, 'Perhaps you and me could change places, then the doctor wouldn't have problems.'

'I'm sure sorry, Miss Lomas,' Holden put in quickly. 'I'll not take my eye off the trail again until I set you down in Kremmling.'

There was no reply from Kate Lomas, and he heard her shuffling back to her station at the rear end. Betsy Gray just grunted and edged away to hold onto the side rail.

An hour later they ran out of a canyon, and at the end of a long grade the huddle of wooden buildings that was Kremmling lay before them.

'Is that it?' Betsy Gray asked without much enthusiasm.

'I guess so,' Holden replied. 'It seems they're expecting interesting company. Look! The word's out the stage's in sight, they're streaming out of buildings onto the sidewalk.'

It was true. The stage was still halfway down the grade and both sidewalks were bulging with humanity. Betsy Gray groaned audibly. 'There's no way we can dodge that lot!'

Kate Lomas was leaning over the roof-rail again. 'Halfway up Main Street on the left-hand side, Mister Holden, that's the stage-line office.'

Mark held his hand aloft to let her know he'd heard her instructions, and he drove into Kremmling to the cheers of the gesticulating crowd. As he pushed on up Main Street the crowds on the sidewalks dropped to the roadway and Holden pulled up in the space the crowd had left opposite the stage-line.

Four men stood on the steps to the sidewalk, all slicked up and dressed in their best. Many hands pushed them down the steps with shouts of encouragement. 'Go get 'em Hank!' someone yelled. 'Which of you lucky hombres gets the purty one up front?' another shouted. A few men noticing Mark Holden asked, 'Where's Dave? What's happened to Lomas?'

The crowd's curiosity proved too much for them and there was a surge of humanity towards the stage. Holden could see that things could quickly get out of hand, and his overriding concern was to get Dave Lomas safely home and his wound properly attended to. Tying the reins he palmed a gun and fired a couple of shots into the air. The crowd froze and everyone stared at the driver, who now stood on the driving seat, his gun wisping smoke.

'Now listen good you hombres!' he yelled. 'Back off! There's a wounded man on this stage who needs attention, and these young ladies are too tired for any celebrating today. They're going to a hotel. This time tomorrow will be time enough to get acquainted. So just let 'em pass into the stage-office.'

The four men dressed in their best looked mutinous, but a lot of the others laughed at their discomfiture, and soon enough, good humour crept back into their features, and ready hands reached for the wounded Dave Lomas. Holden looked up at Kate Lomas who was checking on the cases atop the coach. 'Where do we take your pa, Miss Lomas?' he shouted.

She pointed to the staging-depot. 'We live on top!' she yelled above the general hubbub.

Holden dropped to the ground, and opening the passenger door, climbed in to check on the wounded Lomas, who was now obviously in pain. 'Soon have you comfortable, Mister Lomas,' he said. 'Now while I'm gone you ladies stay right here. If you leave the coach these hombres will forget you need to rest up and nobody'll prise you away from 'em.'

'Thank you, Mister Holden,' one of the girls answered. 'We're not mixing with that lot until we're good and ready.'

Willing hands helped Holden get Lomas safely into the depot and upstairs to his room, and Mark made the man comfortable before hurrying back to the stage. Kate Lomas had a number of helpers to take the cases belonging to the girls to the hotel, but two money satchels she handed to Holden.

'You take these inside and hold on to 'em like your life depends on it,' she ordered. 'That's the month's payroll for the mining company, that's what all the shooting was about. I'll take the girls around the back entrance of the hotel an' fix them up with a couple of rooms. Joe will look after the team.'

Holden held back a quick reply and grasping the satchels stomped his way up the steps and into the office. Whether or not she realized she was treating him like the hired hand. He would have to do some plain speaking to Miss Lomas soon.

Two men followed hot on Holden's heels, and as he stopped alongside the long counter one of them reached for the handle of a satchel. 'I'll take care of that, feller,' he said.

Holden turned and looked into the face of a gimlet-eyed man with a whipcord-strong, six-foot body. Mark resisted the man's attempt to take the satchel. 'If it's all the same to you, Mister, I'll hang on to these until Miss Lomas tells me you've got a right to 'em.'

'I'm Mayhew, Paymaster and Deputy Manager of the mining company, Mister, and what you're holding is what I've come for. You just tell Miss Lomas I've taken what's ours.'

'It don't matter a hill of beans to me who you are,' Holden replied. 'It'll only take a few minutes for the transaction to take place all nice and official. So why don't you park your weight on a seat and sweat it out?'

The man's expression became even more frosty and his companion, a burly, hard-looking man appraised Holden sneeringly.

'You sure like living dangerously, Mister,'

19

Mayhew said at length, then catching sight of the counter-clerk straightening up from behind the counter. 'Hey Dorgan! Tell this blamed fool to hand those money-bags over, he's asking to get himself salivated.'

Mark Holden gave the speaker a cool look, then crossed to the counter and the clerk handed the freight card down from a hook. He pointed out the line that showed the two packages for the mining company. 'You can give 'em to Mr Mayhew,' he said. 'He'll sign for 'em.'

Holden hefted the satchels onto the counter. 'You give 'em to him,' he growled. 'I don't work for the blamed stage-line. Just tell Miss Lomas I'm doctoring her pa.'

Mark was about to go through the inner door when Mayhew called after him. 'You, Mister! Whether you work for the stage-line or no, next time I tell you to do something you do it pronto or I'll put some holes into you.' Mark turned full on to face the man, and he saw the killer light in Mayhew's eyes, and a wolfish anticipatory smile on the face of the man's companion, and his inborn stubbornness rose to the surface.

'Mayhew,' he said quietly. 'My profession is doctoring, and all the time I'm repairing the damage done by loudmouths like you, but if pressed I can dish it out with the best. So you make your mind up, because no matter where or when you tell me to do something, I won't be doing it, and that goes for your sloppy-faced sidekick as well.'

The grin went off Mayhew's pardner's face to be replaced by cold fury, and without regard to Mayhew, he went for his guns. The man was fast, his guns clearing leather with professional speed, but he still pitched to the floor with a hole in his forehead, and Holden was covering Mayhew with a smoking gun. There was no fear in Mayhew's expression, but surprise showed plainly enough. He had never seen anyone beat Mike Slemen to the draw before.

'Being a doctor an' all,' Holden was saying. 'If some blamed fool forces my hand into gunplay, I always make sure I don't give myself any work. So if I were you, Mayhew, I'd get your pard where he can get tidied up for burial.' With that he pushed through the door and made his way upstairs to attend to Dave Lomas.

TWO

When Holden entered Dave Lomas' bed-room, the stage-owner was protesting weakly as a big, motherly-looking woman was dragging at his trousers preparatory to putting him to bed. 'For God's sake, Hannah, leave it along,' he was saying. 'The doctor feller's coming, he'll see to me. It ain't decent, us only being friends.'

'Too right, Dave,' the woman answered. 'It ain't decent, especially the way you look at me sometimes.' She gave a triumphant tug, and faced Holden with a cheerful grin as he walked in. 'You the doctor?' she asked, and as he nodded he could see there was deep concern in her eyes despite the grin.

'Yeah, my name's Mark Holden, and I'd be obliged if you'd rustle up plenty of hot water. I've only patched him up so I want to do a good job on him now. Perhaps if you'll watch what I'll be doing you'll be able to fit new dressings later on.'

'I sure will, Doctor Holden, and Hannah Lord is sure proud to shake your hand for the way you've already helped the old sour-face.'

She made to leave the room, then turned.

'I thought I heard a shot just before you came up, was there any trouble?'

'Yeah, there was. Mayhew, the mining company's man and his sidekick were prodding me some, so I guess I had to kill his sidekick in self defence.'

Hannah Lord looked at him aghast. She had a dozen questions on her lips, but she shrugged her big shoulders and hurried out of the room. The questions were quickly taken up by Dave Lomas when Mark crossed to the bed, and in between the questions Dave managed to say, 'For Pete's sake get me out of the rest of my things and into bed before that danged woman gets back in here.'

Holden smiled and expertly he got the stage-owner into bed, then he cut away the bandages, and removing the pads, surveyed the wound. The bullet had gouged a large chunk of flesh, ploughed through a muscle and chipped a bone. Altogether it was a nasty wound and Dave Lomas would have been due a lot of pain if it were not for a healing resin that Holden always carried, as did his father who had learned the secrets of the resin from a Comanche medicine-man.

Hannah had brought in a bowl of hot water and some towels as Dave Lomas said, 'That was Mike Slemen you killed, Holden. Dan Mayhew and Slemen have been pardners a long time, and there's no way you're going to keep a whole skin with Mayhew

24

after your blood.'

Holden was thinking of something to say that would take the worry out of Lomas' tone, but the door burst open and the dust-covered Kate Lomas crossed the room to look sharply at her father before nodding a welcome to Hannah Lord then casting a look of distaste at him.

'Did you have to get so all-fired uppity that a man had to die?' she asked.

Mark turned away deliberately and when Hannah placed the bowl on a cabinet beside Dave, proceeded to clean out the wound carefully. The stage-owner gritted his teeth as the pain shot through him. Hannah Lord watched closely and Kate, swallowing her chagrin, moved into a position where she could see what was taking place. It was the first time she had seen the extent of the wound. She had been planning on driving the stage herself until the next wages-run, but it was clear to her now that Dave Lomas wouldn't be climbing aboard the stage either to drive or ride shotgun for a couple of months at least.

'Where are my cayuses?' Holden asked as he bent over his task, bringing the girl out of her abstraction.

'They're being stabled out back, and your gear will be brought up to the next bed-room. I take it you don't object to staying here?'

'I'm obliged to you, Ma'am,' he replied. 'It'll be just as well for me to be near for the next couple of days. After that it'll only need careful dressing, and I guess Hannah here is looking forward to that chore. No doubt you've got a doctor if it should become necessary?'

Hannah Lord sniffed and Kate gave a snort of disgust. 'Yeah, we've got a doctor, and if you need him before the saloons open up, he does a good job, but if he's had an hour with the bottle, then you're unlucky.'

'I guess you'll have to watch that he doesn't get into the saloon then,' Mark replied.

'Any reason you can't stay on?' Kate asked.

'I don't have to give you a reason, Ma'am,' Mark said as he spread resin over two thick pads ready to apply on the wound.

'I – I didn't mean that the way it sounded, Doctor Holden,' Kate said in a quiet voice. 'What I should have said is that if you fancied staying in Kremmling for a while, you're welcome to put up here, and we'd be happy to pay for your time and treatment as you think fit.'

Mark made no immediate reply but instead, concentrated upon the job of placing the resin-covered pads where they would do most good, and bandaging them in place. When he was satisfied he looked down at the white-faced Dave and smiled encouragement. 'We'll leave that alone for a day, and see how it goes,' he remarked. 'I'm going to give you a drink of something that'll keep you sleeping most of the time.'

'I'm sure obliged young feller,' Dave Lomas said. 'It's feeling easier already. And thanks for taking sides today, we were in a load of trouble, and Kate would have had her hands full with those hombres breathing down her neck.'

'I'd have handled my end of things,' Kate put in quickly. 'But I'm glad you were on hand, and I'm more glad you turned out to be a doctor.'

As Holden searched for the medicine phial and a small glass amongst his kit he shot a quick look at the girl, and sincerity shone out of her eyes. Finding the articles he sought, he poured out a measure and handed it to the stage-owner, who drank it down with a grimace. Dave Lomas' face took on a relaxed look, and soon his steady breathing indicated he was asleep. Hannah Lord looked at Holden and smiled at the effect of his treatment. 'I expect you'd like to get cleaned up some now, so I'll put you plenty of hot water in the room, and when you're freshened up I'll have a meal going. The same goes for you too, Kate.'

Holden nodded his thanks, and Kate crossed to the older woman and hugged her momentarily without saying anything, giving Mark a glimpse of the femininity of the

27

girl who tried hard to present a tough, masculine attitude to her problems, and he felt some concern for her.

'I can answer your question now, Ma'am,' he said. 'I was passing through, heading for St Louis. I guess it'll take me about five weeks, and in eight weeks time I take up my job as scout and doctor for a wagon train bound for California. So, the most I can spare in this neck of the woods is two weeks. That will be time enough to make sure your father will recover, but not long enough to get him fit for work.'

Hannah had turned back from the door. 'We'd be obliged if you'd take care of him for the next two weeks, Doctor Holden, ain't that so, Kate?'

'Yeah, sure,' Kate said quietly. 'But we can't expect him to take chances on not arriving at St Louis on time. All sorts of things can crop up in that distance to steal away a week or so.'

Holden saw that Kate's face was set in serious lines, and it was clear to him that she was worried. He had a feeling she and her father had never sought anyone's help before. 'I've done the St Louis run a few times,' he said at length. 'And I can stay on a couple of weeks without causing me problems. So if you'll set my keep against any help I can give your father, Ma'am, I reckon you've got a deal.' Hannah Lord went on her way, satisfied.

Kate's eyes gleamed a little as she replied. 'Thank you, Doctor Holden. I'm sure you'll set him up fine in that time. Hannah keeps an eating-house a few doors along, but she has a few Chinese helpers who can look after things while she stops here. Wild horses wouldn't keep her away while my pa is sick. They've been rowing at each other for years, but they're mighty close. Anyway, she'll see that you eat well while I'm away with the stage.'

'You'll get a driver then?' he asked.

She shook her head. 'Nobody wants that chore. I'll drive myself; it's only when we bring in the mining company wages that we need a shotgun rider.'

Holden said nothing, but he looked again at the girl's lissom figure and tried to picture her handling the six-horse team pulling the stage. There was more to Kate Lomas than met the eye. He stood up and started to make his way to the door. 'I'll get myself spruced up,' he said, then stood to one side as the door opened, and a lean, clean-shaven man of about forty-five, wearing a sheriff's badge stood in the doorway.

'Come on in, Sheriff,' Kate called out, and the lawman stepped into the room. His eyes took in the sleeping stage-owner, Kate and Holden all in one glance, but his eyes stayed on the latter.

'You the doctor fella?' he asked.

'Yeah, and the name's Holden, Mark Holden.'

'How's Dave making out?' the lawman asked.

'He'll mend given time, should be as good as new in about eight to ten weeks.'

'Glad to know it.' The sheriff's voice was brittle. 'More than can be said for Mike Slemen, he's gonna be dead for keeps.'

'That's a chance a hombre takes when he goes first for a gun,' Mark remarked sourly. 'You trying to make a case he was hard done by?'

The sheriff looked at him levelly. 'The way I heard it, Slemen went for his gun because your insults didn't leave him much choice. You may be a doctor, but in my book you're a gunslinger, and Kremmling can do without you.'

Mark Holden felt the temper rise in him but he appeared calm when he faced the lawman. 'If you're telling me to move on, Mister, I've just promised to stay for a couple of weeks to take care of old Dave, and that's what I aim to do.'

'We've got a doctor,' the sheriff snarled.

'Now listen here, Sheriff Rudge!' Kate expostulated. 'Doctor Holden saved the stage today from robbery at the least, and drove the stage when my pa couldn't drive any further. Mayhew and Slemen had no call pushing him. The way the counter-clerk told

30

me, Mayhew was lucky he didn't get the same treatment as Slemen. Believe me, I'm thankful that the doctor is as handy with a gun as he is at his own craft. I want him to stay here! Because Doctor Knowles is never sober enough to do his job. So, anybody pushing Doctor Holden will have to watch out for my gun as well.'

Sheriff Rudge looked from the girl to Holden, then shrugged. 'I guess a couple of weeks ain't so long. Just keep outa trouble, Doc.'

'You can take it from me, Sheriff, I won't be looking for trouble. Life's too good to waste.'

The sheriff nodded and touching the brim of his hat to Kate, he went out, closing the door behind him.

'That was mighty nice of you, Miss Lomas. You sure gave me a good recommendation.'

Her glance just failed to meet his. 'The least I could do,' she replied.

Mark tried to think of something else to say then gave it up, and went through the door to his room. Kate Lomas stood staring at the door he'd closed. Doctor Holden was getting to her.

Holden found his gear alongside his bed, and two large jugs of hot water beside the washbowl on the wash-stand. He shaved and washed away every vestige of trail dust out of his skin, then changed his linen, leaving himself feeling refreshed and ready to face the world. As he stepped outside his room he could hear pans and crockery being moved around, so he looked into the dining-room where Hannah Lord was setting places. 'I'll go out back and take a look at my broncs,' he said. 'I won't delay you any.'

'It'll be all of half-an-hour before I'll be ready,' she replied, 'so take your time.'

He took the backstairs to ground level and crossed the paddock to the stables, passing the stage-coach which was being cleaned by a cheery-faced, husky youngster of about sixteen years. His horses were in the two furthest stalls from the door, and when he got level with the stall that held Chief, the big bay stallion, a punchy oldster was just putting the finishing touches to his grooming. The oldster turned to eye him, and grinned a welcome.

'This your cayuse?' he asked and Holden nodded.

'Yeah, I call him Chief, and my moniker is Mark Holden. I'm obliged for the work you've done on him,' Mark glanced at the next stall, noticing that his packhorse gleamed from cleaning and brushing. 'The other one too,' he added, jerking a thumb in the direction of the packhorse.

'Think nothing of it,' the oldster grunted.

'My moniker's Joe Hollins, Miss Kate told me how you horned in today, and how you're a doctor an' all, which is lucky for old Dave, so it's little enough I've done in return.'

Holden smiled and shrugged his shoulders. 'It was just lucky I happened to be passing I guess, although Miss Kate's no slouch with that shotgun. She tells me she'll be driving the stage until her pa gets better. Has she driven it before?'

Joe Hollins glanced sharply at Holden, and there was a big grin on his face. 'You've no call to worry on her account, Mr Holden, she'll handle any team you can string together, an' I guess stage-robbers won't try again until the next payroll run, or the silver consignment out of Kremmling.'

Holden nodded, he was about to go then changed his mind. Kate and Dave Lomas interested him, and it suddenly became necessary to find out all he could about them, and whose hands may be against them. 'Tell me, Joe, have you got any ideas who would be at the back of an attempt to steal the payroll?'

Joe Hollins pushed past Chief a couple of times fixing a feed into the manger without saying anything, then he came out of the stall and fetching a couple of boxes, turned them up on end, sat on one and motioned Mark to use the other.

'It's not easy to say, Mister Holden.'

Mark interrupted. 'Call me Mark.'

'Like I was saying, Mark, it's not easy to say. There was a time when everybody knew everybody. Folk started out together from back east, heading for the west coast. We were a mite late starting out and got snowed under right here, then when late spring came along, old man Kremmling decided to stay put, and nobody else fancied leading the way west. So they dug in here and most folk worked out a reasonable way of life. They had time for each other, and everyone helped when someone came against more problems than he could manage.' Joe Hollins took time out to light a thin cheroot, then continued. 'Then a couple of years ago the mining company moved in. They took over all the holes that most folk worked in their spare time, and the tradesmen were squeezed out. The only free traders left are Dave Lomas and Hannah Lord. Three ranches operated within twenty miles, but there's only one working now, ramrodded by Rod Denning for the Company.' Hollins ground the cheroot out under his heel before winding up. 'So, anybody can be at back of anything in this hyar burg nowadays. One more thing, old Dave Lomas is the only one who's kept his claim tax paid, keeping his claim valid. They've tried to buy him out, but he won't sell. I reckon they'd like to take the stage-line over too.'

'How about Sheriff Rudge? Is he a

straight-shooter?' Holden asked. Joe Hollins gave him a long look.

'He's a Company man, voted in by Company votes, mind he keeps a tight rein on things in Kremmling, but while he seems fair in his dealings the Company comes out on top every time.'

'Who's the boss of the mining company?'

'Henry Bowden,' Joe replied. 'I've never seen him close to. Spends all his time away from the mine workings at the HB ranch, where he keeps a string of pure-bred Lippizana horses.'

Holden nodded and stood up to join Chief in his stall and make a fuss of him, then he did the same with his packhorse. Joe Hollins watched approvingly. As Mark made to take his leave Joe held his arm. 'Just one thing, Mark, all of the mining company's managers are mighty fast to the draw, and they don't hold back any.'

'Thanks, Joe. It always pays to know what's what in any town one intends to hang around in for a week or so. I'd better get back inside for the meal Hannah's getting ready.' He made his way inside the house and upstairs, entering the dining-room ready for whatever was creating the appetizing cooking smell, but he was totally unprepared for the difference in appearance to the girl who had ridden shotgun.

Kate Lomas was a picture of beauty that

had Holden staring. She was dressed in a neat simple yellow dress that in no way detracted from her figure, and her hair of spun gold, shoulder-length, glinting wherever the lamplight touched, surrounding the satin-smooth skin of a classical face, with hazel eyes that returned his gaze with equal interest.

She didn't permit her fleeting thoughts to take root as she dragged her eyes away, but the picture he presented stayed in her mind, she found his dark, sun-burned face, deep-set blue eyes and crisply-curling black hair made her want to take another look.

Kate resisted the temptation and went to see how Hannah was progressing, while Mark took a seat beside the big fireplace and lit up a hand-rolled cigarette. The way Kate had looked remained with him, and it seemed even more incongruous that the girl should be driving the stage-coach on the hard run from Kremmling to Granby. He pushed the thoughts away, there was little he could do to help beyond taking good care of Dave Lomas for the next couple of weeks.

When Kate finally returned to the dining-room she was followed by Hannah Lord pushing a laden trolley, and he moved to the table to sit opposite the girl. Their glances met, and for some unaccountable reason their ability to converse dried up. Fortunately, Hannah was in no way inhibited, and she kept up a lively discourse until it was time for Holden to take a look at Dave.

When he was sure that the stage-owner would stay comfortably asleep through the night, Mark excused himself and sought his room, eager to sleep in a bed for a change.

THREE

Holden woke up at his normal time in the morning but he restrained the impulse to get up in favour of luxuriating in the soft comfort of the bed. Pictures of Kate Lomas floated in front of him in dust-covered range-garb, and in the neat, yellow dress of last evening and he had to struggle to thrust the pictures away. Then he remembered Betsy Gray and he grinned at the memory. The other three women he remembered more as a colourful background to Betsy than individuals. He decided he'd like to be on hand when they got to meeting the men who had paid their passage from St Louis. Remembering Betsy, he reckoned there was no way she would be able to contain her curiosity regarding her potman. He had asked for a full day's grace for the women, but he had no doubt that Betsy would jump the gun.

With the thought in mind he got up, and after a good wash made for the dining-room. Hannah Lord had just arrived and looked approvingly at Mark before busying herself with the coffee pot. 'Dave's still sleeping,' she said. 'It doesn't look as if he's moved all night.'

Mark grinned. 'I'd reckoned on that, it's a mighty potent knockout that medicine packs. Only thing is, it can't be used too often, it's best used at the beginning to help with shock and give a man a good sleep under his belt after an accident.'

'It was a good thing you were on hand, Doctor Holden,' Hannah averred. 'Doctor Knowles would have done his best, but he can never get his mind away from a bottle of bourbon long enough to do a good job.'

Hannah gave him a mug of coffee then shortly afterwards she placed in front of him a breakfast of bacon, eggs, kidneys and fried bread. He found himself glancing towards the door now and again for Miss Kate to make her appearance. Hannah noticed and smiled, brought her own breakfast to the table and set about it with a gusty appetite.

'I guess Kate will lie in today like always,' she said idly. 'She needs all the rest she can get if she's got to drive that durned stage six days on the run.'

'It's not the work for a girl,' Mark said decisively. 'I guess a day behind a team of six spirited cayuses is enough to send a strong man looking for his bed.'

'Nothing you say is going to make any difference,' Hannah said tartly. 'There's very little a man can do that Kate can't do better. The way I see it she's got the best of both worlds. There's mighty few men could best her and she's prettier than a picture when she's got the chance to scrape off the trail-dust.' Hannah was watching his reaction closely but Holden's expression was non-committal, and Hannah was left wondering which of the two attributes the doctor disagreed with.

Holden stood up at length and Hannah looked at him questioningly. 'I'll take a look at Dave so's I can figure out when he's likely to wake up, then I'll take a look around town, and maybe the mining company's workings.'

Hannah nodded, then as he reached the door she called after him. 'You'll need to keep a sharp eye to your back if you're trailing around town. There's a lot of folk hanging around Kremmling who don't rate other people's lives much.'

He smiled at her. 'I'm not looking for trouble so nobody should be wanting to prove anything with me.'

'Mike Slemen had plenty of cronies,' Hannah said drily.

Holden's eyebrows lifted, then he nodded. 'I'd figured he used to spend his time at the workings with that hombre Mayhew.'

'Mayhew and Slemen were always good for free drinks and handouts to some Kremmling folk who passed them information they could use to advantage.' With that Hannah stood up and started gathering up the used crockery and Mark passed through to the room where Dave Lomas slept like a babe.

Later he passed through the stage-line office and stepped out onto the sidewalk. There were plenty of loungers around, propping up doorframes and leaning on the sidewalk rails, but none of them spared him more than a glance as he walked the entire length of town, then crossed the dusty road to the opposite sidewalk to idle his time looking into stores. Kremmling followed the pattern of most small towns, and there was little enough to commend any of them; Kremmling just had less than most. At length when he was opposite the Crippled Wagon Hotel where Betsy Gray and her companions were staying, he crossed the road and entered the saloon section.

There were a few customers dotted around the tables, all perking up to face the day with the dog's-hair drink safely tucked away, and the same cheery-faced youngster he had last seen cleaning the stage-coach was sweeping around the tables. Holden walked up to the long counter, and the barkeep who had been stacking cases behind the counter stood up and eyed him expectantly. Mark noted the steady, blue eyes, the crinkly, brown hair and the massive shoulders as the man smilingly awaited his pleasure.

'Beer, please,' Mark asked, then as an aid

to conversation added, 'And have one yourself.'

The barkeep filled two glasses and after wishing Holden 'good luck' he leaned across the bar, studying his customer. 'You're the doctor feller who drove the stage in for old Lomas yesterday. That right?'

Holden agreed before taking a tentative sip of beer. 'Yeah, the name's Holden.'

'Glad to know you, Doctor Holden.' The barkeep thrust his horny hand across the counter and as Holden shook it firmly, he added, 'My moniker's Dale Webb, an' I'm obliged you lent a hand when that stage was attacked.'

'The Lomases mean something to you eh?' Holden questioned.

'Oh yeah, Dave Lomas an' that hellion daughter of his are fine, but there was a little lady on that coach I'm due to wed.' His face clouded over. 'Trouble is I don't know which one of 'em. You got a bit promiscuous with the lead and set the introductions back for today sometime.'

Holden grinned at Webb's aggrieved expression. 'I guess those ladies were a mite tuckered up after the journey and the excitement of that attempted stage hold-up. They were a bit hot-tempered an' outspoken by the time we hit town. I'd say they were in no mood to meet prospective husbands.'

Dale Webb's eyes lit up with interest.

'That's the way I like 'em, a bit spiky. No woman ever came spikier than my old lady but she was pure gold right through. I figgered out for myself she only spoke her piece because she cared a lot.'

'That's plain good sense, Dale. Anyway your Miss Betsy Gray's outspoken enough, even though she looks like butter wouldn't melt in her mouth.'

Webb's eyes widened. 'How in heck do you know Betsy Gray's my intended?' he asked.

'She said she'd set out from St Louis to Kremmling to get wed to a potman. I guess that's you. She was the little lady who sat alongside me when I took over the driving.'

'You mean the little purty one?' And when Holden nodded Webb had a faraway look in his eyes. 'Well, I'll be hornswoggled!' Dale Webb emptied his glass in one to celebrate the news, then his expression became pensive. 'I guess I'll have to change my job, there's not enough free time in bar work to suit a purty new wife.'

Holden's glance went straight to the barkeep's powerful shoulders and immediately he pictured Webb handling a team of six with panache. He decided to test the barkeep's interest. 'I'd reckon there's not much you couldn't handle once you'd set your mind to it, Dale. You ever thought of driving a stage?'

'Nope, can't say I have, but I've handled all

sorts of teams carting timber from the slopes of the Appalachians to the mills for the railway company.' He paused and looked thoughtful. 'There's never been a call for a stage-driver here, but now with Dave and Rube out of action I guess it only leaves Miss Kate. Yeah, I guess if I had one run alongside Miss Kate I could take over right enough.'

Mark nodded, satisfied. 'I'll see what Miss Kate's got to say, Dale.' He pushed his glass across the counter for a refill, and passed a coin over. 'And I wish you luck when you meet up today with Miss Betsy.'

'I sure appreciate yore help, Doctor Holden.'

Before Mark could make any comment a couple of oldsters hammered their table with an empty bottle, so Webb took down a bottle of rye and crossed to the table. When he returned he nodded towards the oldsters. 'The hombre with the black coat an' big white moustache is Doctor Knowles. That's his second bottle. Durned if I know where the old coot puts it.'

'I reckon I'll have to do something about Doctor Knowles before I leave this neck of the woods,' Mark murmured. 'He's not living up to his professional promises.'

'I dunno 'bout that,' replied Dale, 'but they say, after they get him sobered up he does a mighty good job.'

Holden nodded before making his way out

via the hotel section. As he pushed through the door Betsy Gray reached the foot of the stairs. She had brushed the trail dust out of her clothes, and scrubbed herself clean as a new pin, presenting a picture of delicious femininity. Her eyes lit up at the sight of Holden.

'Well now, you're sure a comforting sight,' Betsy said, her frank gaze showing wholesome appreciation.

'Glad you find it so, Betsy, but there's no call for you to be looking for comfort in Kremmling. I reckon you'll have very few regrets if you keep to your bargain.'

Betsy's face showed surprise. 'You're full of surprises, Doctor Holden; doctor, stage-driver, gunman, an' now a match-maker. It looks like you've met the man who paid for my ticket.'

Holden smiled. 'Yeah. I met him, Dale Webb's his moniker, that right?'

When Betsy nodded, Holden pushed the door to the saloon open, and looking inside, he caught Webb's attention and waved him over. Halfway to the door the potman caught a glimpse of the dress behind Holden and his pace slackened, apprehension spread over his face, then Mark saw him mentally square his shoulders and pick up speed again, and a moment later Dale and Betsy were eyeing each other. Holden broke into the silence and Webb's embarrassment. 'I guess it's my privilege to be acquainted with both of you so, Mr Dale Webb meet Miss Betsy Gray.'

They shook hands and Betsy appraised Webb frankly, Dale stammered a bit as the girl's beauty made him feel inadequate, but at last he managed, 'I – I sure hope you'll like things here enough to want to stay, Miss Betsy. It – it's gonna be a few hours before I get some time off to show you around an' get to talking things out, mebbe you can find something to do 'til then.'

Before Betsy could think of a fitting reply Holden broke in. 'If you'd like to look in the stage-office when you're through, Dale, I'll take Miss Betsy to see Miss Lomas, they'll find plenty to talk about. I can see about the stage-driving at the same time.'

As he spoke there was a hammering on the bar counter for attention, and Webb muttered his thanks to Holden before dragging his eyes away from Betsy's lovely face and pushing backwards through the door. Betsy was left staring at the door for a moment, her expression thoughtful, before turning to Holden.

'Well, Mister Holden, I guess I'd better do like you say for today, but I'll be making my own mind up whether or no Dale Webb's worth staying for. He ain't repulsive or anything, but there's a lot of things he is that could take me too long to get used to.'

Holden laughed at her typical forthright

remark, and taking her arm, they stepped out onto the sidewalk; it was a short distance to the depot but every male eye was on her and murmurs of appreciation rose to a volume that left her in no doubt of her attraction. She kept her eyes straight ahead or on her companion, and that is how Kate Lomas saw them from her father's window.

Kate had just satisfied herself that her father was all right, and was taking a look at Main Street before going to the next floor for a late breakfast. Hannah Lord was at the door that linked the kitchen and gave her a greeting.

'Take it easy a while, Kate. I heard you moving around and I've got your breakfast nearly ready.'

'Thank you, Hannah. It's real good of you.' She went to pick up a six-month-old catalogue when there was a quiet tap at the sitting-room door. Kate crossed the room and opened it, then stood staring at Doctor Holden and Betsy Gray. Anger came into her eyes and her thoughts tumbled around. 'This doctor hombre sure enough had gall. One night in town then he brings in his pickup for breakfast.' She found herself standing aside as Holden ushered Betsy Gray inside.

'This is Betsy, Miss Kate, she's just met her intended, Dale Webb, but he'll be tied up for a few hours, so I thought you'd put her wise to things in Kremmling.' He paused a moment while Kate's frown disappeared to be replaced by a welcoming smile. Then turning to Betsy he continued, 'I bet you never thought Miss Kate would look that way outa that shotgun gear.'

Betsy was first in. 'I thought she looked cute riding shotgun, but she sure looks good enough to eat right now. Er – I don't want to put you to any trouble.'

Kate's eyes spat fire at Mark for his temerity in drawing attention to the way she looked but the fire had gone when she turned her attention to Betsy. 'Come right on in and make yourself comfortable.'

Hannah Lord came to the door again, sizing the situation up immediately. 'Can I dish up another breakfast, Kate? It's no trouble.'

Kate looked questioningly at Betsy who nodded without hesitation. 'Sure thing, I could eat a longhorn.'

Hannah turned away with a grin. She liked forthright folk, and a little later she took in coffee for the three of them, whereupon Kate made the introductions. Holden didn't waste much time with his coffee, and when he drained his cup he stood up and made for the door.

'If you'll excuse me I've got a chore to attend to. I'll be back later to take a look at your pa, Miss Kate.' He passed through the door before either of the girls were able to answer, and going down the stairs he went through the depot office and back onto Main Street. A couple of minutes later he was back in the Crippled Wagon Saloon. Dale Webb looked up in surprise.

'I didn't take you for much of a drinking man,' Webb said coolly. And his expression seemed to imply that Holden had feet of clay when he had expected better.

Holden smiled. 'I'm not here for drinking, Dale. I'm gonna do something right now about the way Doctor Knowles attends to his business. Just where does he live?'

Webb's surprise deepened but he answered readily. 'You'll find his shingle on the last building the north end of Main Street. He lives above the surgery, and Bertha Todd cleans up an' cares for him.' Dale dug for a cheroot as Mark walked towards the table where Doc Knowles had pushed his glass to one side, and was taking his rye straight from the bottle.

Doctor Knowles found his bottle yanked out of his grasp. He looked owlishly at his empty hand, then his blood-shot eyes fastened on Holden's midriff and travelled slowly upwards to settle on his face. Holden looked hard and mean but Knowles was in no condition to define what an expression boded, and he made a lurching attempt to reach the bottle that Holden held, but Mark moved the bottle out of range then picking up the cork, rammed it home, turned on his heel and returning to the bar, handed it over to Dale. Doctor Knowles struggled to his feet and staggered his way to the bar. With the counter to steady him, he hauled himself straight and after a couple of attempts to compose himself, managed to steady his gaze on Holden.

'What in heck do you think you're doing? You give me back that durned bottle or I'll put a hole in that hide of yours,' he mouthed.

'You've done finished with that or any other bottle, Doctor Knowles! The next drink you take you'll be able to handle without it stopping you doing what you promised to do whenever your skill was needed.'

Holden was going too fast, and Knowles was finding it difficult to concentrate. Mark turned to Webb briefly. 'I'll see to him from here on,' then whipping out a gun, he stuck it into Knowles' ribs, then grasped the doctor's collar with the other hand and propelled him to the door to the hotel section and out onto the sidewalk.

There was a fair crowd on the sidewalk and they stopped in their tracks to stare at the medico struggling in the grasp of the young newcomer. Holden holstered his gun and held onto Knowles breeks because he was now supporting the doctor's weight, and as he trundled the man onto the road to cross to the other sidewalk the volume of noise increased on the street as men called the attention of others to the spectacle.

The noise reached the room above the stage-depot where Kate Lomas and Betsy Gray were making inroads into their breakfast. Kate crossed to the window and stared at the sight of Doctor Knowles squirming in Holden's clutches. Betsy saw her expression and hurried to her side. 'What in tarnation does he think he's doing?' mouthed Kate, while Betsy said, 'Ain't he just a humdinger?'

His intention was too obvious as Holden turned to his left. A horse-trough stood between him and the next steps, and he had his eye on it.

'Oh no! He wouldn't!' Kate exclaimed.

'I reckon he will,' Betsy prophesied. And sure enough he did. At the trough Holden picked the doctor up bodily and dumped him without ceremony into the water.

Doctor Knowles disappeared from view, then appeared gasping and spluttering, his moustaches and hair lying flatly over his face. Holden pushed him under again, and after Knowles had re-emerged, he ducked him for the third time.

Sheriff Rudge pushed his way through the crowd and his eyes lit up at the opportunity Holden seemed to be providing to stamp his authority. 'Hey! You Holden! Back off an' leave the Doc alone.'

Holden half turned, taking in Sheriff

Rudge's hard-faced stare, he kept his hand on the doctor however, completing the treatment. 'This is doctor business, Rudge, an' there's no call for anyone else to horn in. This hombre ain't keeping to the promises he made when he got the right to put up his shingle. Well I'm gonna straighten him out some.'

'A man's got a right to do his job the way he sees it,' Rudge said evenly. 'Now back off!'

A mean look came into Holden's face. 'Well it don't work that way for doctors. I intend to see this crittur looks after the folk of this town the way he should if I give him this treatment every time he turns into a saloon.'

Rudge's stance altered and Mark noticed the signs.

'I told you to back off, Holden!' The sheriff's hand was sneaking for his gun as he spoke, but he would have been a lifetime too late if Mark had fired. Rudge let his hand drop to his side, staring as though hypnotized at the forty-five that pointed unwaveringly at his heart, and there was an audible gasp from the onlookers.

'Unhitch that belt, Rudge, an' kick it over to me, or I'll put a slug into your hide an' leave the patching up to this hombre.'

The sheriff's eyes were pinpoints of hate as he did what he was told, and his face was almost apoplectic when Holden holstered his gun, and sweeping up the belt, dumped it into the trough. Then Holden helped Knowles out and led him onto the sidewalk and on towards the man's surgery and home. Wide-eyed and grinning, folk fell away and at last Holden had the man in the care of Bertha Todd.

Bertha accepted the situation calmly; Knowles had come home in all sorts of conditions and nothing surprised her any more.

'I'll be along to see him right soon,' Holden told her. 'Get him dried up an' in between the sheets an' he shouldn't come to much harm. I'm gonna make a doctor out of him again or drown him. It's up to him I guess. Anyways, if he slides to the bottle I'll see he takes plenty of water with it.'

FOUR

The two girls eyed Holden uncertainly when he eventually returned, but he looked as calm and unconcerned as if he had played no part in disturbing the peace. The breakfast things had been cleared and Kate and Betsy had been busy finding some common ground for conversation.

When it became clear that Holden had no intention of mentioning the fracas, Kate couldn't leave it alone. 'I saw what you did to Doctor Knowles, and Sheriff Rudge; do you always set out to make enemies of everybody whenever you hit a town?'

Mark smiled, making his face crinkle in good humour lines, and both girls lost interest in the answer as they studied his handsome face. 'Nope,' he replied. 'In most places folk hardly notice my passing, but Kremmling needs a lot of shaking up. Doctor Knowles needs to be reminded of his promises; and I aim to help him do that before I leave town. As for Rudge, he had no cause to horn in.'

'Rudge is a dangerous man to cross, Doctor Holden, and I reckon you'd be wise to take the pressure off.'

'When I leave Kremmling I want Knowles to be doing the job he was trained to do; in fact tomorrow he's gonna be here, sober an' ready to patch up your pa.' He paused. 'And now I've got a question that interests both of you ladies.'

Kate shot him a doubtful glance but Betsy's face was bright with interest.

'You were saying, Miss Kate, that you couldn't find anyone to take the stage run to Granby. Well I've found just the man for you, that's if Miss Betsy's got no objection.' Betsy was round-eyed now. 'Dale Webb's done plenty of team-hauling in his time, and he reckons that a lady as pretty as Betsy Gray wouldn't want a husband working pot-man's hours every goldarned day. All he'd want was for you, Miss Kate, to show him one run.'

Betsy and Kate looked at each other, and Mark, watching them, was amazed that they reached agreement without exchanging a word. Just a fleeting change of expression seemed to ask and answer all of the questions, then Kate looked back at Holden. 'When can he start?' she asked.

'I've asked him to call around for Betsy when he gets off duty, so you can ask him then for yourself.' He moved towards the door. 'Well, you coming to see how the patient's getting on?'

Kate stood up to follow him, and Betsy

was right behind her. 'Mind if I take a hand,' Betsy asked, and Kate smiled as she shook her head.

'I guess if pa's awake he'll appreciate looking at you. It'll take his mind off the pain.'

'I bet he's got no eyes for anyone save his daughter,' she replied. ' And I can't say I'd blame him.'

As Mark made his way upstairs he marvelled at the way women changed. Just yesterday, when only a short distance outside Kremmling he had narrowly missed the boulder on the trail, their cutting remarks to each other seemed likely to alienate one from the other for life, yet today they appeared in complete accord.

Dave Lomas was awake and it was plain to Mark that the pain from his wound was getting through to him. Kate was beside him first, deep compassion showing in every line of her face. 'How're you feeling, pa?' she asked.

Old Dave forced a smile on his face. 'A bit sore I guess,' he answered. 'But nothing I can't handle.'

'I'll take a look at things as soon as somebody rustles up some boiling water,' Mark commented, and when Betsy said she'd look after that chore, he continued. 'Who do you think those hombres were who tried to rob the stage yesterday?'

'I didn't get a look at 'em when they

opened up, but for my money they're mining company men. They want me out for two reasons, the stage franchise and my claim. They want to run their own shipments an' my claim's stopping 'em expand their workings the way they want.'

As Dave was talking so Mark had started to remove the bandages from his wound, stopping as a grimace appeared on Dave's face. 'Am I hurting you much?' Mark questioned, but Dave shook his head.

'No more'n I'd expect,' he answered. 'I've just remembered what I'd planned to be doin' tomorrow,' he groaned. 'I was gonna ride to Denver to pay the claim tax. If it's not paid on the nail, they can reclaim it an' you can bet the Company'll have some hombre there ready to pay up.'

'You relax, pa,' Kate put in quickly. 'I'll ride in and pay the tax.'

'You're gonna drive the stage tomorrow, Kate, so how in heck can you get to Denver? Goldarn it, those hombres knew they only had to wing me an' it'd all fall into their hands.'

Betsy came in with the hot water and Mark carried on taking away the bandages and dressings from the gaping wound. He studied it and pressed gently around it, and although Dave squirmed a bit he gritted his teeth against the pain. Then Holden sponged the wound before reaching into his bag for a pot of resin and spread some resin onto pieces of bark which he took out of a side pouch. Placing the bark, resin to the wound, he padded it up and replaced the bandages.

'It'll only get better from now on, Dave,' he said. 'But it'll take time, so I guess you're gonna need some help to sort your problems out. Your franchise will be safe if you take on Dale Webb to do your driving, an' if you'll let me have your claim tax I'll ride into Denver, it'll only take me four days.'

Dave Lomas' eyes opened wide, his pain momentarily forgotten. 'Why in heck should you be taking up my problems?' he asked, and Mark grinned.

'Because it's only you and Hannah Lord who've had the gall to buck the mining company and the crooked law. I guess you deserve any help you can get.'

Words seemed to fail Dave Lomas and his head sank onto the pillow, his eyes screwed up to hide his feelings at having his troubles lifted from him.

'It's enough that you're staying long enough to get him on the way to being as good as new,' Kate stated. 'I can get to Denver in time if Dale Webb's going to do the second run on his lonesome.'

'He's not gonna be on his lonesome, no siree,' Betsy Gray said before Mark could say anything. 'I'll be on the end of that shotgun. I was filling the pot for a family of workers when I was no more than knee high to a coyote.'

'Good for you, Miss Betsy,' Holden said with a warm smile, which seemed to set a frown on Kate's forehead, then turning to Kate, 'I'll guarantee to have Doc Knowles doing his job so your pa won't miss me when I ride to Denver, and now, if you can leave him to the care of Betsy and Hannah and show me the mining company's holdings and the HB ranch I'll be obliged. I like to know what I'm up against.'

Kate looked to Betsy, who nodded, then swallowing words that tumbled into her mind, she shrugged her shoulders. 'I – I'll get myself changed.' Her hazel eyes settled on his face, and she had to struggle to keep her interest under control. 'Will you tell Joe to get my cayuse ready?'

'Sure thing,' Mark said, and with a grin at Betsy, he left the room for the stables.

A short while later Holden and Kate set out and headed west after clearing the north end of Main Street. Mark allowed the girl to take the lead but after a few minutes she reined in her Palomino and waited for him to come alongside. 'Which do you want to see first, the mining company or the HB ranch?'

'I'll leave it to you,' Mark replied. 'I guess you know best.'

She looked across at him in some surprise,

60

but stifled back the first reply that came to her mind. 'In that case we'll take a look at the mine first.' And she gigged the Palomino forward before easing to the south-west.

They were soon in rolling, hump-backed country, and ran through a succession of shallow canyons before coming to a steady rising gradient, leading to a plateau that stretched a few miles before arriving at an escarpment where the side of the hill fell away steeply to a mile or so of flat country. Beyond, a forbidding-looking mountain rose solidly to about six thousand feet behind a huddle of foothills. Plumb in the middle of the central foothill, puffs of steam indicated the presence of a haulage engine, the distance making the engine-houses look like boxes.

'That's it,' Kate said as they sat their mounts sufficiently far back from the escarpment so that they would not show up on the skyline.

Holden nodded. 'Well, let's get down amongst 'em, then you can show me your pa's claim.'

Kate immediately set her mount to the steeply-sloping hillside and Mark followed close behind her. Reaching the bottom of the grade they rode in silence until the workings of the mine company was no more than two hundred yards distant. A narrow, fast-running stream curved with the foothill, and

Mark suspected it turned south at the next hill.

Men were moving around the buildings, manhandling tubs as the stationary engine drew them out of the black hole that had been driven into the mountainside, and guiding them towards a screening plant, where metal-bearing ore was separated from rock, and a hill of waste showed up away to the north.

It didn't take long for interest to be shown in the presence of the two riders, and after a while the man Mark knew to be Mayhew stood in the middle of a group, staring across. He made a sharp gesture to the man standing alongside him, who walked away. A few minutes later the man returned, leading a cayuse. Mayhew climbed astride the animal and fording the stream stopped a few yards away from Mark and Kate.

Mayhew was dressed for the mine. A rough, hair shirt tied at the neck with a knotted 'kerchief, and moleskin trousers disappeared just below the knees into leather leggings. He carried no guns, but his eyes held a menacing quality.

'Just so you'll know, things have changed some, Miss Lomas. The other side of that stream is mining company land, an' the road belongs to us. I guess you'll have to use the other way in from the south.' His face split in an evil grin. 'It's no more'n twelve miles.'

'You don't have to take that hombre's sayso, Miss Kate,' Holden said evenly. 'You'll need to see the claim map signed by the land agent of the Denver office first, then you can take it up with the Land Registry Commissioners.'

'I've warned you before, Holden, to keep outa things that don't concern you. Anyways I've told you, an' there's a dozen rifles pointed in your direction if you've a fancy for trespassing now.'

Holden laughed, and took time out searching for the makings and building a cigarette. Kate shot him a surprised look, and Mayhew was momentarily puzzled. 'You enjoy your temporary superiority of numbers, Mayhew. It's not going to last much longer. You've used your weight to more or less steal the claims you're hogging, and you've driven out traders from Kremmling. Well, like I said, enjoy it while you can.'

Mayhew had recovered his poise. 'If what you said was true, Holden, there's nothing you can do to alter things, so fork your freight.' He turned his horse abruptly, and rode away stiff-backed.

Holden found Kate staring at him, her face angry. 'Things are bad enough as they are, Mister Holden. Why in Hades do you have to talk through your blamed hat to make things worse? Where are you going to get more men than the mining company have got on their payroll? If there were men with enough gall to tackle those hoodlums they'd have done it before they lost out everything they owned.'

Mark merely smiled. 'It never hurts to sow doubts, and considering that Mayhew intends to pick his own time to force me to the draw the more doubts I can make chase around his brain the better.'

The anger left Kate's face to be replaced by concern. Mark was about to set his stallion on the move but Kate's hand was on his arm, staying him. 'There's only one reason why I wanted you to stay and that was to get my father better. There's no call for you to take sides in our troubles. The best thing is for you to do what's most important, an' that's nurse my father back to health. The stage-line franchise isn't all that important, and the claim's not worth the sweat.'

Mark shook his head as he gigged his mount to the west. 'There's no way I can turn back now. I've got to bring things to a head before I'm due to leave for St Louis.'

They rode for some time in silence, clearing the foothill where the mining company worked, then through a canyon that split the next foothill and then south-west, following a well-marked trail that Mark guessed led to the HB ranch headquarters.

Eventually Mark broke the silence. 'Er, those hombres who got forced out of business, are they still in town?'

Kate considered for a few moments. 'Yeah,' she replied. 'For the most part they're taking a wage for working in the places they owned.'

'Mebbe you'll ask Joe Hollins to sound 'em out about joining in driving the Company out?'

'I don't know,' Kate said. 'I'll have to think about it.' And Mark had to be content with that.

They rode for another hour or so, both lost in their own thoughts. Kate thinking of the man who rode just ahead of her. Mark Holden interested her because he was so unlike anyone she had previously met. He was a doctor, yet he was an outdoor man, hardened in the way of the trail-blazer, even now, with the prospect of leading a wagon train on the perilous journey from St Louis to the west coast, ready to help out folk who were strangers to him. He was outspoken, fearless and ready to fight at the drop of a hat. She found herself staring at his broad shoulders and thinking unmaidenly thoughts.

Holden was riding ahead because he found Kate Lomas disturbed his train of thought. She filled her clothes in such a way that he had difficulty in keeping his eyes on her face, and when he managed that he found her beauty had him staring. Mark tried hard to push considerations of his companion aside so that he could give his mind to ways of sparking the hotbed of feelings that lay uneasily just below the surface between the mining company and the tradesmen they had ousted and cheated.

He breasted a hill and looked down at a wide, long valley, with a river running along its length, fed from the massive range of mountains that rose just beyond the last couple of foothills. On a knoll stood the HB headquarters, square and solid, and spread around the main house were sundry large buildings; beyond them, big paddocks, each holding a few horses.

'That's Bowden's place,' Kate said, as she brought the Palomino alongside him. 'You'll find he'll have plenty of gun-happy hands within calling distance, so don't push him. I've heard he don't rate lives very high. Other people's lives that is.'

Later, when they started up the side of the knoll, they saw five men fanned out across the trail at the top. 'That's Rod Denning the HB ramrod in the middle,' Kate said quietly. 'They don't come tougher, and those four hombres are always alongside him, ready to back his play.'

As they got close, Holden had to take a harder look at Denning to try matching his appearance with Kate's description of his character. The man appeared to be in his late twenties, slim-built, blond with crisply curling hair, a big smile permanently lodged on his face, showing strong, white teeth, and star-bright blue eyes. The four men ranged alongside him seemed out of one mould. All were burly, black-visaged, hairy hulks, dressed in cowhand garb.

The five men stepped back sufficiently far to enable Mark and Kate to breast the top of the hill, Denning's companions had their hands close to their six-guns. Holden reined-in and eyed Denning interrogatively. 'Where's your boss?' he asked.

A film seemed to form over Denning's eyes, and although his smile was still intact, the blue of his eyes was gone and they now seemed slate-grey and menacing. 'The boss don't make a habit of talking to every hombre who rides in.' His voice held a sneering quality, and he was watching Mark closely for his reaction. 'I guess he leaves me to handle things, so if you've got a problem you can spill it to me.'

'Nope. You just tell Bowden that Mark Holden wants a few minutes of his time.'

Denning's eyes narrowed, and the men alongside him shifted a bit as they took closer stock of Holden. 'So, you're the hombre who salivated Mike Slemen?'

'I didn't have any choice. The blamed fool went for his shootin' irons,' Mark replied. 'What's your moniker anyway?'

'The name's Denning, an' I ramrod everything for Mister Bowden except the mining side, so, say what you've got to say an' I'll tell you what you want to know.'

'I guess you've jumped to the wrong conclusions, Denning. What I need to discuss with Bowden concerns mining only, so either stand aside while I look for him or let him know I want to talk.'

Denning's smile slipped a little as he realized he'd outsmarted himself, but he shrugged his shoulders and pointed to the big building next to the ranch-house. 'You'll find him in there,' he said, before turning away and heading in the other direction, his acolytes falling in closely behind him.

Holden eased his mount forward and rode up to the ranch-house hitchrail just ahead of Kate. They dismounted and after tying the animals to the rail, crossed to the next building. They pushed the door open and looked inside to find that the building held two long lines of stalls, and between the rows of boxes was a wide, long, sawdusted schooling area. A man stood beside a beautifully muscled, white Lippizana stallion, and was discussing the animal with a wizened dwarf of a man who was moving around the horse with the confidence that came from close daily contact.

The larger man turned away and came to the doorway. 'Howdy, Ma'am,' he said, tipping his Stetson to Kate, then facing Holden.

'Well?' Mark took his time to study the man before taking up the invitation to talk. He was tall, well knit and exuding authority.

'You Bowden?' Holden asked at last, and the man nodded, coolly.

'An' you, from the description I had from Mayhew, must be the doctor who killed Slemen, er, Holden, ain't it?'

'Yeah, an' there's just a couple of questions I'd like you to answer,' Mark said quietly. 'Is it right you've bought up the land so that the Lomas claim can't be entered from the north end, and you're insisting anybody working the claim'll have to make the twelve mile detour? An' are you behind the hombres who attacked the stage and shot up Miss Lomas' pa?'

Kate gasped at the directness of Holden's questions, but if Bowden felt any sense of irritation he failed to show it.

'Yeah, it's true I've bought the land clear from the mine to where the road joins up with the Kremmling Stage route, but it needn't bother Mr Lomas none. I'll pay him a good price for that claim of his, so he'll be saved the chore. Mind, that offer only holds if he pays the tax on the claim in time.' He paused. 'Now, as to the stage hold-up. I never yet gave a man an order that would set him outside the law, Holden, but any mining company attracts all sorts, and I can't say some of 'em didn't make a try for some easy money.'

'If you'll ask around it could be easy to prove,' Mark put in. 'I winged three of 'em. Mebbe someone's covering for 'em.' When Bowden nodded, Mark continued. 'As to the claim, I'll be heading for Denver tomorrow to settle the claim tax business, and it could be I'll get your ownership of the land that closes his entry set aside, seeing his was the first claim registered.'

Kate was muttering to herself as Mark hogged the conversation, but considering he was merely stating the truth of things, she realized she had no real cause for anger. Bowden for his part was thoughtful. He was getting the impression that Holden could cause him problems, so characteristically he appealed to the baser instincts by putting forward a proposition.

'I've heard you've started trying to make a doctor out of Knowles. Well I pay him a retainer to attend the mine if needed, but if you'd like the job I'll pay more'n you'll earn anywhere else; think about it and we'll talk.' With that Bowden tipped his hat again and hurried back to the Lippizana. Mark and Kate returned to their horses and set off on the return journey.

FIVE

Kate was thoughtful as she followed Holden to the foot of the knoll. Bowden gave the impression of standing outside the actions of his minions, as though he held no responsibility for the way they rode roughshod over everyone, yet he professed himself ready to pay a fair price for her father's claim, so disclaiming any attempt to force him out. She looked at the straight-backed young doctor just ahead of her, and wondered whether Bowden's gold would turn him from the intention of setting things to rights in Kremmling, and from moving on to guide the wagon train west. She wondered why he had told Bowden of his intention to ride to Denver on the morrow to keep the claim alive. They were halfway to the next foothill when she decided to get things cleared.

'You going to get yourself on the Company's payroll?' she asked as she brought her Palomino alongside him. Holden glanced across at her, and seeing the frown on her face a smile etched his lips.

'I guess I'll know better when Bowden starts talking money,' he replied, watching the frown deepen, and anger sharpen her gaze. 'He's gonna have to pitch in pretty high to top what I'll make taking the wagon train to the West Coast.'

She edged her mount away from him and looked straight ahead as she spoke. 'So you're ready to go to the highest bidder? I guess I'd formed the wrong impression, Mister Holden; I didn't think money mattered the most in your scheme of things.'

Mark said nothing and Kate dropped back to stare savagely at the man who had so suddenly appeared to have fallen from grace. It had seemed he was getting to grips with her father's problems and was about to get things back on an even keel; but now his motives were suspect, he was probably after the biggest dollar.

They climbed the hill, topped the rise, then when just below the rim of the escarpment Holden reined in and slid out of the saddle. Kate rode on a short distance, then after a few minutes returned to within fifty yards or so, and stayed watching him curiously.

He undid his saddle-roll, taking out a blanket, then he set to searching for kindling wood. It took him about twenty minutes to collect enough for his purpose, and during this time he spared no glance for the girl.

Setting some of the kindling wood alight within a ring of stones, he fed it carefully with rooted tufts of grass. In a few minutes he had the fire under control by feeding just the fibrous roots of grass, and smoke rose steadily in place of the flames. He collected the blanket and when he moved alongside the fire he stole a glance in Kate's direction. She was watching in wide-eyed incredulity.

Smoke soared skywards in puffs and circles, the intervals varying between puffs and between successions of puffs bearing the same interval, and the smoke rings changed in size and density, then after five minutes activity Mark withdrew the blanket, and after replacing it in his saddle-roll tied the roll back in place. He returned to the fire and sitting on his heels proceeded to make himself a cigarette, his eyes sweeping the ridges of the massive mountains behind the last couple of foothills.

Kate closed the distance and slid from the saddle, ground-hitching the Palomino, she came alongside Mark and sat down.

'I guess I've seen everything now,' she said. 'You're the first hombre I ever saw sending smoke signals, an' it's all mighty clever, but what you hope to get out of it beats me. I thought it was only Injuns who understood 'em.' Her words tailed off.

'My best friends are Indians,' Holden said simply. 'I've lived close to them most of my life.'

Kate's eyes widened even further with surprise. 'And I suppose you were sending a message to your friends?'

Mark nodded and pointed to distant ridges where smoke erupted in spurts. From a dozen points smoke rose skywards forming practically the same pattern, then died away. Holden took no particular notice but he still stared at the mountains as patient as any Indian. Then he was all concentration as smoke rose from one central point, in a long, complicated pattern for fully five minutes, then he stood up and held out a hand to help Kate to her feet.

'Well, that's it,' he declared. 'I guess we can head for home.'

Kate climbed astride her Palomino, her face alive with curiosity. 'Are you going to tell me what all that was about?' she asked, and Mark nodded.

'Yeah, the Cheyenne will be watching out for me to Denver and back, an' they'll be watching out for the stage too, from Kremmling to and from Granby. So if you see any Indians riding close to the stage don't get jumpy and start popping off that shotgun of yours.'

Kate was unable to grasp why Indians should put themselves to the trouble of wet-nursing white folk, and there was an expression not far from disbelief on her face so Mark started to make things clear for her, and by the time he had explained things and answered her questions they were back in Kremmling.

At the staging depot Kate accepted Mark's offer to stable her Palomino while she checked on the freight list for the next day's run before looking in on her father then joining Betsy Gray and Dale Webb in the big room overlooking the street. Betsy was bubbling with good humour and it was apparent to Kate that she was finding enough in Dale Webb to hold her interest, while Dale was finding it a bit hard to keep up with the ebullient Betsy.

When Kate finally got Dale Webb talking about his team-handling she was soon satisfied that he would fill the bill, and they quickly settled the question of wages.

She had found her father awake but trying to hide the fact he was in pain, and she was becoming restive, wondering what in heck was keeping Mark in the stables. She was about to find out when the street noises rose considerably, and she crossed to the window to divine the cause. Her groan brought Betsy and Webb hurrying to her side. 'Oh no! Not again!' she exclaimed.

Once again Mark had Doc Knowles in tow, dragging him by the collar, and there was no mistaking Mark's intention. Nobody was interfering; the onlookers hollering to friends so they wouldn't miss the fun. Once more the doctor was dumped into the trough, and when he spluttered to the surface Mark pushed him back under and held him for just long enough. Then he hauled him out and dragged the unfortunate man towards home and dry towels.

Bertha Todd eyed Holden without resentment, but there was compassion on her face as she took care of the spluttering doctor. 'I sure hope he catches on to what you're trying to do, Mister. They didn't come better than Doc Knowles a few years ago.'

'Yeah, Ma'am, I'm sure you're right. I guess most of his old friends have moved on and he's looked for comfort in the bottom of a bottle. Well, I'll be calling for him at sun-up tomorrow and he'll spend the day making sure Dave Lomas is comfortable an' on the mend. I reckon between us we'll have the Doc back as good as he ever was.' There was a doubtful look on Bertha's face as Holden took his leave.

When Mark made to enter the stage-depot he had to stand aside to allow four Chinamen bearing covered trays to precede Hannah Lord through the door. He touched his hat to Hannah with a 'Howdy, Ma'am,' and she grinned at him.

'I guess you timed things just right, Doc Holden. You'll be able to get your feet under the table in time to catch it piping hot.'

'I'm sure enough a lucky coyote,' he answered with a grin, and Hannah clumped her way up the stairs, thinking that any effort was worth his sort of appreciation.

Immediately after they had eaten Mark and Kate joined Hannah Lord in Dave Lomas' room. He had eaten everything that Hannah had prepared for him, and although his eyes showed he still had pain, the food had brought colour to his cheeks.

'We'll take a look at things, Dave, then you can give me what I've got to take to Denver tomorrow. I'll have Doc Knowles here, cold sober by sun-up, an' just make sure he gets no more hard liquor than one glass, morning, afternoon and night, then he'll do a good job.'

Lomas nodded, and gritted his teeth when Mark removed the bandages. With the wound revealed Mark pressed and probed around the edges, and at length applied another pack of resin-covered bark to the wound, rebandaged, and sat back satisfied, while Dave gave Kate some instructions that sent her to the desk set alongside the wardrobe, to return with a small, fold-over, leather wallet. She handed it to Mark.

'That's what you'll be taking to Denver to-morrow. The claim needs stamping up once they've got the cash.'

Mark nodded, and taking the wallet stuffed it into an inside pocket. 'D'you think you can separate Betsy Gray from Dale Webb for an hour or so? I'd like to see he gets his time from the Crippled Wagon, and gives me information about Kremmling folk and the mining company men who use the place. I reckon if Betsy stayed close I wouldn't get a word in edgeways.'

Kate smiled and agreed. 'I'll go and arrange it,' and she left the room leaving Mark to spend a few more minutes with old Dave before joining the others. Dale stood up as he entered the room, dragging his eyes away from Betsy with an effort.

'I guess I'm all ready,' he said, and followed Mark down and through the depot onto the sidewalk. 'I'm thinking Josiah Sloan's gonna be riled some at me leaving him short-handed, but that's his headache, he's given me plenty in his time.'

Mark smiled, and reckoned Dale could handle anything his boss might throw. They fell in step, and entering the saloon section of the hotel took a table well away from the other customers. When they sat down they both felt the power of the stare that a grim-faced man directed at them from behind the bar. He moved along to the hinged flap, and thrusting it up, stepped through and made his way to the table. His attention was focused on Webb.

'Where in heck have you been?' he snarled. 'And what in tarnation are you set there for? Get to where you belong pronto.'

Dale looked unabashed. 'Guess you'll have to get yoreself a new barkeep, Sloan. From now on I'll be driving stage for Lomas.' Josiah

Sloan's eyes narrowed and an expression of annoyance crossed his frosty face.

'You must be loco!' he snarled. 'Lomas is on his way out and that's for sure, you're gonna be out on a limb. I'll give you ten minutes to get your palavering done and be back the other side of that bar.'

'I'll take my chances,' Webb said, as Sloan made to turn away from the table. 'You'll find young Walt Maggs can handle a bar-keep's job, so that should solve your problems. One thing though, you owe me a month's dinero, an' I want that before I go.'

It looked for a moment as though Sloan was going to turn nasty, but after transferring his gaze to where young Walt Maggs was collecting up empty pots, he shrugged his shoulders, and turned on his heel to return behind the bar.

Mark followed him and ordered two beers, which Sloan served with very bad grace, and as Mark carried the glass to the table Sloan caught young Maggs' attention and motioned him over with a gesture.

Webb and Mark watched Sloan talking at the youngster for a few minutes, with Walt nodding every now and again, then at length Sloan raised the flap for Maggs to walk through and stand the other side of the counter with a big grin on his face. He caught Dale Webb's glance and the grin widened at Dale's nod of encouragement.

'He can sure use the money,' Webb muttered to Mark, under his breath. 'His ma's got three little 'uns to bring up. His pa got gunned down by Dan Mayhew when he was working his claim after the mining company hit the territory. Jonas was goaded into going for his gun, but he had no chance against Mayhew.'

'Young Maggs won't be doing any more stage cleaning if he's gonna be working full time as barkeep,' remarked Mark. 'So I guess we'll have to pitch in and help. How do you reckon he feels about the jasper who killed his pa?'

'Huh – I know how he feels!' exclaimed Dale. 'That silly grin of his don't signify he's simple, or just glad to be doing something. I've seen him practise and practise his draw until a six-gun flows into his hand like quicksilver. He don't ever wear one in town, oh no, he's waiting until he's grown up some, and fast enough to salivate Mayhew for sure. He hates every last one of the mining company men but I reckon he'll be happy just to even the score with Mayhew.'

'If you asked him to keep his eyes open and to report anything about the movements of the top men, d'you reckon he would?' Mark asked, and when Dale nodded, 'Well, ask him to pass anything on to Joe Hollins. The more we know about 'em the better.'

A couple of minutes later Josiah Sloan

crossed to the table and slapped some coins in front of Dale Webb. 'You'll find it's all there,' he said, before returning to the bar. Then he went through the door to his office, slamming it behind him.

Dale picked up the coins, and went across to hold a quiet conversation with the new barkeep. Mark noticed that the grin had vanished from Maggs' face the moment Dale leaned over the bar, and the eyes that flashed a glance at the table were bright with intelligence.

An hour before sun-up Mark Holden knocked on Doc Knowles' door and waited for signs of life to show. The window shot up and Bertha Todd's shawl-covered head poked out of the aperture. 'It's me ma'am, Doctor Holden,' Mark said in a hoarse whisper. 'I'm collecting Doc Knowles to look after Dave Lomas.'

'Hold there!' Bertha replied. 'I'll put a few clothes on and I'll let you in.'

Her head disappeared and the window was slammed shut, then after about five minutes the light went from the bedroom and Mark heard her clumping down the stairs. He smiled as he heard her withdraw half-a-dozen bolts before getting the door open, then she stood aside to allow him to enter.

'You want me to wake him?' Bertha asked, as she closed the door behind Holden.

'No. Just show me where he is,' Mark replied. Bertha yawned as she nodded her head, and she preceded him up the stairs. Pointing out the room, she handed him the lamp and went into her room.

Mark pushed the door open, and turning up the lamp he placed it on the cabinet before surveying the man who slept like a babe. In repose Doc Knowles looked the epitome of respectability and professional integrity. There was quality and intelligence in every line of his features. When Mark shook him awake all the good points disappeared, and a disgruntled, glowering face stared back at him. Recognition came slowly but when it did, the good doctor's eyes were pin-points of hate.

'What in Hades do you want?' he snarled, reaching under his pillow. Mark's hand closed on his wrist, and with the other hand he drew out the heavy Colt and held it with the muzzle against Knowles' temple.

'I want you now, cold sober and ready to be a doctor over at the stage-depot to look after Dave Lomas until I get back.' Mark's voice was cold, detached. 'Just get up, dress, and don't try anything smart.'

Knowles' face became frozen as his brain grappled with the implications; the thought of a day under the threat of this young maniac without the prop of copious draughts of bourbon was almost too much to bear, but he wanted no more of the water-trough, and with a muttered curse he thrust the bed-clothes aside and reached for his clothes.

SIX

Kate Lomas woke up as Mark Holden passed her bedroom door on his way to fetch Doctor Knowles. She had slept very little, having lain awake thinking mostly of the young doctor, and what he had told her of his life among the Indians, and once again she allowed the words to run through her mind. 'My father turned from his own kind when I was just two years old. He was away helping a neighbour's wife in childbirth, when three ruffians hit town. They saw my mother in town and followed her home; when they left they had used her and beaten her to death. Not one man raised a voice against them as they rode off, and no one could give my father a description of them. The moment my mother was buried my father put me and his belongings into his wagon and headed west. He found a valley in the Cheyenne mountain country that was sheltered even in the worst weather, and he stayed, and in time became friendly with the Cheyenne. He passed on his knowledge to the medicine men and gave them the credit for the results of his skill. He learned their language and taught English to Indian children and any brave eager to learn. Running Wolf insisted that all his chiefs learned the white man's language; I was always at his side, and he taught me everything in his power, including medicine.'

He had paused at that point and Kate had pressed him to tell her more, so he had continued. 'Well when I was about six I pulled Running Wolf's daughter out of the river when it looked likely she'd end up in the white water, and from then I was treated as a blood member of the Cheyenne and all the Plains Indians who were by then forced to live in the mountains. While my father taught me everything he knew, I was brought up Indian fashion, playing, fighting and competing with the youngsters of my age, and except when in my father's house, I spoke nothing but Cheyenne, Sioux and other Indian languages. Before I changed from boy to man I had to seek the dream the Great Spirit sent and every dream showed I'd have to be a medicine man. So my father decided I'd have to train the way he did, and when I was seventeen he fixed for me to join the medical college in Boston. Well I got my Doctor's Diploma, and a better knowledge of white folk which decided me to take out a few years, getting to understand them better. I found a lot of good whites while scouting the way and looking after them through the Rockies to California; yeah, as good as any

Indian, but too many of 'em were ready to kill at the drop of a hat. I guess to live amongst 'em you've just got to be faster to the draw.' She went over it again and again, staying with it to better understand him, and she wondered about his father, who had done such a good job on the child he was left to care for. She came to with a start when footsteps sounded on the stairs.

After washing and dressing she went into her father's room where Doc Knowles was darting rebellious glances between Holden and the newly-awakened Lomas. Mark saw her and smiled a welcome so she crossed to the bad-tempered doctor's side, grasped his arm and said disarmingly, 'Oh, I'm so glad you're going to be looking after my father, Doctor Knowles. You'll soon get him back to rights.'

Doc Knowles struggled with his expression as he looked at her, and somewhere from the depths his professional pride surfaced, fighting back the impelling urge to get his fingers around the neck of a bottle. 'Yeah, yeah. Don't fret none, soon get him back on the stage. Would have come sooner if you'd asked. What in tarnation made you let this charlatan prod around with things he don't understand?' With a baleful glance at Holden.

'He did a good job, Doc,' Lomas growled. 'An' he was on the spot when it happened.'

'Mm, mm. Well I'll take a look an' see just what he's done.'

'Just one thing, Doc,' Mark stated in a hard, clear voice. 'You stay here until I return. No sliding off to a saloon, an' no more than one glass of bourbon morning, afternoon and night. Any backsliding an' I'll take you into the desert to dry you out the hard way.'

Before Knowles could think of a sufficiently scathing reply Mark left the bedroom to make his way to Hannah Lord's Eating House for breakfast and to order supplies to last him for four days.

He collected his saddle-roll while Kate and her companions were eating and went out the back way to the stables. Joe Hollins was putting the finishing touches on the last of the team that would be hauling the stage on the run to Granby, but before Mark had finished saddling up Hollins was alongside him. They exchanged greetings but the oldster was instantly serious.

'Young Walt Maggs looked in last night, and he told me that Rod Denning and the Dando brothers were in the Crippled Wagon with Sheriff Rudge an' planning to stay the night there. From bits an' pieces of talk he was able to pick up he reckoned that Denning and his sidekicks were gonna stop you from getting to Denver for a few days. He opined you ought to know to look out for 'em.'

'Thanks, Joe,' Mark replied. 'And next time you see Walt, tell him I'm mighty obliged. I was expecting to meet problems on this chore, but it's handy to know where the trouble's coming from. Anyway, Joe, they'll be out of luck so don't lose any sleep on my account.'

Hollins looked doubtful, for his money Rod Denning and the Dando brothers meant trouble in a big way, and he couldn't see that one man stood much chance of holding out against them. However, he concluded he wouldn't help any by casting doubts on Mark's ability to come through with a whole skin, so he turned away, muttering, 'Well I'd better hitch 'em up and get the stage around front.'

'I'll lend a hand,' Mark remarked, and together the two men led the animals outside and got them hitched up. 'Nothing wrong with these critturs,' Mark said at length as Joe held onto the reins and clambered aboard.

'The best,' Joe replied. 'They're a straight cross from Morgans and a British breed, er – er.' He scratched his head, searching for the name. 'Oh yeah, the Cleveland Bay. I reckon they've got the best of both breeds.'

Mark nodded, and Joe clucked and shook the reins and the horses took the strain and moved off at an easy pace. Mark climbed astride his bay and followed slowly, keeping out of the dust.

Joe pulled up in front of the depot and tying up the leaders, entered the office, and a few minutes later Dale Webb emerged carrying a miscellany of articles for delivery at Granby. Mike exchanged grins with him, and Dale stowed the articles away and returned to the office for more, reappearing and followed closely by Betsy Gray and Kate. Betsy carried a shotgun in a way that suggested she could use it if necessary and Kate was armed to the teeth.

The two girls caught Mark's eye, and while Betsy grinned widely Kate's glance held a lot of reserve, yet Mark sensed a hint of anxiety in her expression, and it set him to wondering whether or not the anxiety was on account of the timely arrival at Denver of the claim renewal. Betsy climbed atop and settled herself and Webb was just about to tell Joe Hollins to untie the leaders when two men came abreast on the sidewalk with hands raised. Hollins paused and waited for them. They were sleepy-eyed gambler types, carrying small, leather holdall bags, men who travelled light. The nearest to the rail caught Dale's eye.

'Hold on there a minute pardner, just so's we can buy tickets for Granby.'

Dale glanced at Kate who nodded, and the driver growled, 'Hurry it up then.'

Both men smiled and turned into the

office. Mark kneed the bay alongside Kate and motioned her to listen. She leaned towards him, and after he'd whispered at her, she climbed down and stood in the road.

The men reappeared and climbed one after the other into the coach. They sank back into the wide seat with satisfied grins when Mark's gun preceded his face through the road-side window. They stared in surprise, then their expressions hardened as he spoke.

'Now take it easy an' do just like I say, that's unless you want to stay in Kremmling for keeps. Reach nice and easy for every bit of hardware you're carrying an' toss 'em on the floor against this door. You'll get 'em all back when everything's been checked in at Granby.'

With bad grace the two men did as they were told, neither of them prepared to chance going for the little Derringers in their shoulder holsters.

Mark slid to the ground, pulling the door open and keeping his gun on the passengers while Kate reached inside the coach and collected the guns. Slamming the door shut, he kept an eye on the men until Kate took her place beside Webb who told Hollins to untie the leaders. Then with a shout from Dale the stage moved forward, accelerating to spew up dust along the length of Main Street.

Hollins looked up at Mark who had regained his place on the saddle. 'What was all that about?' he asked.

Mark shrugged then smiled. 'Can't say for sure. But there was no time to ask about 'em so I reckoned it seemed sense to draw their teeth. There's no harm done if they're on the level.'

Joe Hollins nodded agreement, and stepped aside as Mark raised his hand in salute and set the big stallion moving down Main Street. Joe watched horse and rider take the south trail, and the worry lines showed on his face as he saw Rod Denning and the Dando brothers emerge from the Crippled Wagon and line the side-rail until Mark Holden disappeared around a wall of rock, then, unhurried, the five men headed for the livery.

Right from the time he crossed the Colorado River Mark knew for sure he was being followed. It was his sixth sense at work. No sign had come from his Indian friends but they would warn him soon enough if the men dogging his trail got close enough to threaten him.

A tight smile etched his lips as he edged his mount off the trail and set it to a fairly steep slope, passing after about fifteen minutes between two rocks that stood like giant sentinels. The terrain had become rugged, and always rising, so the men at his heels were due a lot of discomfort before they closed the distance enough to cause him any mischief.

He stopped beside a fast-running, mountain stream, and allowed Chief to drink sparingly of the ice-cold water, then to pick at the sparse grass along the bank, while he ate his way through one of the packs Hannah Lord had provided. When he remounted, he pulled his slicker around him tight after covering his face up to the eyes with his bandanna and pulling down the brim of his Stetson, then he murmured to the horse, 'Well, Chief, the next six hours is gonna be the worst; let's get it done.'

The big bay turned its head and one dew-soft eye rested on Holden as though taking account of his rider muffled to the eyebrows then soon they were into the snow, and in next to no time visibility went almost to nothing as a fresh snowstorm raged around them. The stallion lowered its head against the elements but kept going without hesitation; Chief never forgot a trail, and snow or no snow, Mark knew the animal wouldn't put a hoof wrong.

The huddle of riders pulled up and stared at the evidence with misgivings. Rod Denning swore loud and long. He opined out loud that the trail was bad enough so why in

Hades should anyone head for the distant snow-covered peaks? The Dando brothers offered no reasons, but their faces registered sullen anger. They continued to stare at the sign that showed where Holden had left the trail, but Denning had switched his sights to the steep side of the mountain, picking up the two sentinel rocks standing close together. He swore again as he drew his conclusions.

'There's nothing for it but to follow this jasper,' he snarled. 'We took him to be a stranger to this neck of the woods, but it looks like we were wrong. Our plan to keep him at Mungo's place west of Idaho Springs is a dead duck, it's my bet he knows a way to Denver before this trail would get us to Idaho Springs.'

The Dando brothers stared up the face of the towering mountain then back at each other. They looked rebellious. Frank, the eldest, spoke up for all of them. 'Soon as we get that hombre in our sights we'll put a slug in his hide. There's no way I'm gonna fork my cayuse up there.' His brothers Sam, Henry and Will growled their agreement, and Denning, whose decision to delay the capture of Holden until they reached Mungo's shack was responsible for the man being still a free agent, shrugged his shoulders.

'Well let's get going. We'll salivate him then return to the trail and head for Denver to fill in the claim for the Company. With luck nobody'll find him; Rudge won't be looking, that's for sure.'

The swirling snowflakes made visibility nil, and both horse and rider were covered with a thick coating of clinging snow. Holden was hunched in the saddle always seeking for sight of the mountain wall that spelt safety, while the horse, head low, kept inexorably on, slowly but unhesitatingly, and always climbing. Then, as quickly as it had started, the snowflakes thinned and stopped, and soon the snow was reflecting a myriad pinpoints of light from the sun. Man and rider shook themselves free of snow and Mark stared back down the face of the mountain and backtrail. Remembering the terrain, he reckoned this would be the last time he'd get a view of the entire face. Very soon he'd be entering the inner mass, corkscrewing his way in and up, ever up. Despite the sun it was bitterly cold and he was thankful for the body heat of Chief.

He was about to restart when he saw the moving dots far below. Squinting in the dancing sunlight he picked out five horses and riders which he added up to mean Rod Denning and the Dando brothers. Even as he watched, he saw the smoke rising on a ridge below the snowline of the mountain the other side of the trail. There was a pause, then the message rose clearly enough. 'The five men had followed him all the way from Kremmling, and White Eagle would be keeping close.' He turned Chief in a full circle to show he'd received the message, confident that sharp eyes would pick up his answer and pass it on. As he urged Chief forward he reflected upon his good fortune in having such good friends; he grinned as he thought about the word friend. White Eagle and he had pommelled the living daylights out of each other throughout childhood and early manhood, yet they had always grown closer.

Ten minutes later and the thin trail moved inside the mountain wall which towered up over in a perfect windbreak, and the cold became less intense. The slope was still there, steep in places, but the going was better. Every now and again they emerged on the side of the mountain to turn back into it when an opening showed, and Holden was now taking careful stock of his position.

At last he arrived where he intended to turn the table on his pursuers. He had noticed with satisfaction that no new snow had fallen at this level and the surface was impacted as hard as flint. There'd be no sign to follow at this point. The wall of the mountain separated again with apparent trails each side of the wall, and just before the separation an opening apparently led back into the mountain. The mouth of the opening was not high enough to permit both horse and rider to enter, so Mark dismounted and led Chief deep inside. The horse remembered the place, and waited patiently while his master checked outside for sign, and used a blanket to smooth the dust at the entrance.

The tunnel made a couple of sharp turns effectively blocking out the light which came from an ever-widening crack above them to where the inner wall opened out, and for a long time the trail was sheltered. When it emerged onto the mountain-side Holden looked back to his left and eyed the wide expanse of snow that ran thousands of feet down the mountainside. He knew full well that the two trails he had left in favour of the fissure opening both ended at the top of that smooth expanse, and underneath the thin mantle of snow was a glacier and nothing to hold onto.

Leading Chief back into comparative shelter, Mark helped himself to another pack of Hannah Lord's sandwiches and tried estimating how long it would take the five men to arrive at the glacier. He reckoned at least an hour and a half so he chanced a cigarette and sat down to wait.

Rod Denning rode with the constant cursing of the Dando brothers in his ears, but he was well used to their grumbling and made nothing of it. When it came down to cases he could depend on them to do as they were told, and quickly. They had ridden a long time together and gathered plenty of dinero on the way. He understood the reason for their grumbles lay in the fact that they never bickered between themselves, so they embraced every extraneous reason to vent their spleen. As he drew his slicker closer around him Denning reflected upon the fact that he'd soon be parting company with them. They'd soon be gathering a trail herd together for Kansas City, and only he knew how many beeves would go under the hammer under his own name. He'd see the Dando brothers right, but he reckoned to ride away with a sixty thousand dollar stake, and still keep the mining company happy. The trail herd would be more than twice the size Bowden believed when it finally cleared the Anvil territory on the easier northerly route for Muddy Pass through the Divide.

He jerked his mind back to the chore in hand and looked up at the uncompromising face of the mountain; there was no sign of Holden, and he swore to himself. Another five minutes and they'd be into the snow. He felt sore at having this particular chore. Holden was riding on mining business and Bowden had no call to get things mixed. Mayhew should be clambering up this blamed mountain, and he should be rounding up his beef, savouring the profits.

When they hit the snowline their spirits were low. The chance of a rifle-shot simplifying their chore was gone. They now had the awesome task of following a man who obviously knew every inch of the route over the Divide. Denning glanced upwards and he shivered involuntarily as he saw the cloud covering the peak. He was a man of the Plains and would make a detour of fifty miles quite cheerfully rather than tackle a mountain, but now he had no choice. No matter what conditions awaited them before they hit level ground the other side, they had to put up with them if they were going to stop Holden getting to the claims office in Denver on time. The Dando brothers were too disgusted to give voice; they rode with chins tucked into their chests, following their leader with a similar lack of enthusiasm. They too were Plainsmen, and hated the high, rugged snow country. Will Dando in particular smouldered with resentment. If Denning had listened to him, they'd have crowded on speed and salivated Doc Holden long before he had got to the foot of this durned mountain. Eventually he shrugged his resentment away. Mostly Denning was right, so Will reckoned he had no call to allow this one mistake to rankle. Not questioning Denning's sayso added up to a lot of kudos and very little hard graft. It also kept the brothers together.

By the time the pursuers reached the point

where the mountain face split to create a windbreak they were frozen to the marrow. The wind had increased and seemed to consist of slivers of ice, making each man aware they had not made proper provision for riding in these conditions. The sight of temporary shelter galvanized the two youngest, Frank and Sam, and they urged their mounts ahead to take cover first. When all five were clear of the wind Frank pulled up and took out a package from the inside of his slicker.

'You hombres can crowd on all the speed you want, but me, I'm gonna get outside some chow, then I'm having me a smoke.'

Denning pulled up. He suspected that the going was going to get worse so this was no time to antagonize the brothers. 'You sure enough read my mind, Frank. It's a dime to a dollar that Holden will take time out to eat, he doesn't know we're dogging him. There's no way of knowing how this blamed trail twists and turns, so by my reckoning we'll not settle his hash until we hit open country the other side.'

So they were in accord when they set off again, but Frank and Sam took the lead. Denning raised no objections; when it came to following sign there was no-one better than Frank Dando.

They kept going, cursing when the trail brought them onto the face of the mountain, and failing to enjoy the occasional shelter out of fear of the next spell of exposure. Inexorably they came to where they had a choice of taking a fairly wide trail that ran around the outside of the curving mountain or inside the wall that sheered up to a crack that let in the daylight. The outside trail showed nothing, so Frank opted for the inside. They all failed to take account of the low cave-like entrance they had just passed.

The trail twisted and turned, with the gap letting in daylight widening until they eventually came to where the outer wall petered out with the trail appearing to continue around the face of the mountain. Snow had built onto the rock floor of the trail and extended around the mountain face giving the appearance of solid foundation. Frank and Sam Dando were already on the impacted snow before the outer mountain wall fell away, exposing the wide sloping expanse at a forty-five degree angle as far as the eye could see. Frank Dando's doubts crowded in as a glance to his right showed a continuation of the vast expanse of sloping snow, and he shouted a warning as he tried to back his mount. He bumped back into Sam's mount at the same time as a loud cracking sound preceded the break-up of the built-up ice from the rock floor, and one after the other Frank and Sam Dando slid away with their screaming mounts onto the smooth surface of the glacier that was only lightly covered with fresh snow.

Rod Denning was next in line, his mount held rigid with its hooves firmly on the snow-covered rock floor. He saw the expression of horror on Frank Dando's face as the man turned and stretched for a handhold before Sam's horse cannoned into him. There were a few seconds when Denning had the tumbling men and horses in sight as their speed of descent accelerated, then they were gone, lost to view. He came alive to movement behind him, and fear crowded in; one push and he'd go the same way. 'Get back! Get back!' he shouted. 'There's nothing we can do! Get back to where we can turn these cayuses.'

Will and Henry Dando had to fight hard against the urge to push forward regardless of the dangers, but Denning's warning reached a corner of their brains, and Will, the backmarker, quickly had his mount backing away. The other two eased back in turn until they all arrived at a safe place, then as one they dismounted, and without a word being spoken each man reached for his lariat and headed back to the edge of the rock-floor.

They fastened each other together with Denning's lariat, and Will Dando took tentative steps almost to where the snow arch had given way, then stretching out full length he got head and shoulders clear of the edge and stared down the face of the glacier. Here and there, bits and pieces of saddlery and clothing littered the face of the ice, articles without the weight or friction to keep up speed or impetus, but of men and horses there was no sign, and Will Dando eased himself back with bitterness in his soul. Standing up he turned to his brother, Henry. 'They're gone! And we're not going to find 'em neither; but one thing we're gonna do, an' that's cause Holden more trouble than enough before cashing his chips for him.'

Henry Dando said nothing, but the expression on his face said it all as he turned away to return to where their mounts waited. Rod Denning made no comment. Now wasn't the time to give orders to the Dandos. There was nothing for it but to return and report to Bowden that Holden had carved himself too much of a lead.

SEVEN

Mark Holden used the time that he sat alongside his cayuse mulling over the situation in Kremmling, and the means by which he could bring about a rude change in things during the time he was able to spare. When the hour and a half was almost up, he made his way to the vantage point that overlooked the glacier, and by then he was satisfied that provided he'd get the right answers to a few questions, he should leave on time with the job done. Another half-an-hour passed with his mind shying from consideration of actually leaving Kremmling, and a wry grin appeared on his lips as his thoughts kept switching to Kate Lomas. He shrugged the thoughts away; he doubted if she'd notice he'd gone so long as her blamed stage-line kept raising the dust between Kremmling and Granby.

The screams of fear from Frank and Sam Dando's cayuses focused his attention immediately on the glacier, and a split second later he saw the two animals, quickly followed by their unseated riders, bounce and tumble a few times before sliding at ever increasing speed down the slippery surface.

When the distance took away the edge of shape the mass moved on, to become a dot that finally disappeared. He had registered the faint shout 'Get back! Get back!' and he guessed that even now the remaining three men were easing their mounts away, and doubting the stability of the ground beneath them; they'd be shaken, and for his money they'd pick their way back to level ground and give up the chase.

Any responsibility for the death of the two men Mark dismissed from his mind as he climbed into the saddle to continue his journey. It was true he knew of the danger awaiting the pursuers at the end of either of the two trails; the place was part of Indian folklore, and many a tale had been told around camp fires of the Mountain of Sliding Feet. But there were dangers everywhere, and men who took the sky route should know what to look out for. He was content to have outfoxed Denning and the Dando brothers.

Twenty hours later Holden rode into Denver. He left Chief at the livery, spick and span, and tucking into a well-deserved feed, before seeking out an eating house, then a little later he arrived at the Land and Assay Office.

When Mark crossed to the counter the inner office door opened and a thickset man of about forty-five stepped through to greet him. He found himself looking into two deep-set, steady, grey eyes, set in a strong, weather-beaten face. The man wore a black Albert jacket and Levis that disappeared into ankle-length leather boots. His smile showed pleasure. 'Howdy,' he said. 'Found yourself a goldmine?'

Holden smiled and shook his head. 'Nope, I guess not. Can't say I ever will, mainly because I won't be looking.'

'Well, what can I do for you? If you saw the shingle you might have noticed that my moniker's Henty; Chris Henty that is.'

'Mark Holden,' Mark replied. 'And I'm glad to make your acquaintance. Anyway, I've ridden over from Kremmling to pay the claim tax for Dave Lomas.' As he spoke Mark pulled the leather wallet from his inside pocket and laid the contents on the counter.

Henty nodded as he reached for the claim agreement. 'Lomas,' he mused. 'That's the oldster who runs the Kremmling to Granby stage?'

'Yeah, that's so,' Holden agreed. 'He got shot up when some hombres tried holding up the stage. He was carrying the mining company's wages.'

'I heard about it,' Henty said, then he looked sharply at Mark. 'Er – Holden you say?' Then when Mark nodded, 'So you're the doctor who took a hand an' ended up salivating the mining company gunslinger, Slemen?'

'Yeah, he had it coming.' Mark looked hard at the assay man, trying to gauge where his interests lay, but the man's reply and the way he said it made it clear he had opinions of his own and wouldn't be guided by interests.

'All mining companies come to the same pattern,' he said quietly. 'They flood into the nearest town in droves and in no time they take over. Any man who stands against them gets to Boot Hill sooner or later; you've made it in time to keep the old man's claim going for another year but I'll lay a dime to a dollar the Company'll be running the stage before the tax falls due again.'

'I wouldn't bet on it. In a running fight that stage carries some mighty mean defence,' Mark said, then he qualified it by adding, 'Still there are plenty of ways to run a hombre out of business, and that mining company's sneaky enough to know all of 'em.'

Henty nodded as he reached for a shelf behind him to take down a book of payment forms. He opened it out and spread Lomas' claim document to enter up details.

'One thing bothers me,' Mark said quietly, 'is why the mining company's been given sole use of the road to the workings from the Kremmling to Granby stage run. That gives Lomas a twelve-mile detour to get to his workings.'

Henty looked up, his eyes bright. 'They

haven't bought the land yet. They've applied, and I've sent on the application to the Indian Agencies. So until they get the agreement the Company's out of order stopping anyone using the road.'

Mark Holden stared at the assay man, a puzzled look on his face. 'Can I take a look at the map you work by?'

'Yeah sure,' Henty replied and, turning away from the counter, rummaged through dozens of rolled maps until he found the one he was looking for. Unrolling the map on the counter he placed paperweights across the face of it. He stuck a large forefinger on the area covering Kremmling, but Mark was looking at the legend at the foot of the map, which gave the key to boundary signs. Indian territory was indicated by red dots. Transferring his gaze he saw that Henty's forefinger was rounded by the red dots. The three big foothills separated by a ten mile wide strip of level ground from the mass of larger foothills that tumbled east to nestle at the foot of the gaunt, precipitous Rockies were marked Indian territory.

Even while he formed a question for the assay man, he was remembering the story passed down by generations of Cheyenne of the hill where the grass grew but no animals lived. They called it the Eagle of Death. Viewed from the east it had the shape of an eagle with wings humped as though protecting young, and throughout the years innumerable potential braves had gone there to await their dream and their medicine from the Great Spirit, and all had either been found dead or too close to death to save. The hill was now taboo and Mark understood why the chiefs had made no war talk about the mining company's occupation.

'How come the Indian Agencies are involved when there's no mention of 'em on Lomas' claim documents?'

Henty gave Mark a level look. 'Because the man I replaced, Slim Tagget, saw a chance to make himself a stake out of his sure knowledge that the Indians would make no trouble. He used a plan showing no boundaries and pocketed the claim money, and continued to do the same until the mining company showed up. He pocketed their first down-payment and rode into the sun, and I had to pick up the pieces. It took me some time to regularize it, and now, any taxes paid to the Government are passed on to the Indian Agencies for purchasing supplies for the Reservations.'

Mark digested this, then when he spoke it was with quiet authority. 'So you've regularized things in money value only, as between white-run departments? The Indians don't know that trading has taken place over their territory? Now one thing is sure, I could put a spoke into the whole thing. There are

Indians enough up in those hills,' nodding towards the Rockies, 'to run the mining company out of the State of Colorado; but for the start, just drop the road concession for the Company and let 'em know pronto, so that when I go looking for Lomas' claim I won't have to salivate any other gun-happy Company man.'

Henty stood up straight and shook his head. 'I reckon I'd better get advice from higher up before I tell the Company anything. These big companies have got powerful friends in high places, an' little people like me can lose out when the big wheels turn.' He paused, sizing Mark up again. 'How come you can stir the Injuns to take a hand in things?'

'I was raised Cheyenne style and I've got a lot of friends spread around those hills. If I asked, I'd have more Indians at my back than most white men see in a lifetime.'

There was a doubtful expression on Henty's face, but Mark's next statement gave him food for thought.

'I knew before leaving Kremmling I'd have Rod Denning and the Dando brothers on my trail, out to stop me getting here on time to keep the claim going. Well, my Indian Pards kept me advised all the way, and I was able to guide 'em onto a couple of trails that either led to death or nowhere. Two of 'em fell through an ice-arch onto a glacier and slid to their death, the others had to turn back to report failure.' Mark smiled at Henty's wide-eyed interest. 'I guess you'll hear about it soon, just like you heard about the stage hold-up.'

'You aiming on starting another Indian War then?' asked Henty.

Holden shook his head emphatically. 'Nope. It could be though, that after I've taken a good look at the hill the mining company's taken over, and explained some things to the Cheyenne, they'll want it for their own use.'

'Well, I sure like your style, Holden, an' if I can help you in any way, just let me know. I've never liked the mining companies, they trample every decent hombre underfoot, like they were no account. If you can move 'em on before they've broken even on their investment I'd sure as heck give you my vote for Governor.'

Henty had stamped up Lomas' claim as he was speaking, and he slipped it into the wallet before handing it over to Mark.

'I've got no political aims, so I won't keep you to that,' Mark said with a grin, as he slipped the wallet into an inside pocket. 'But I'd appreciate a note stating that the road is open to Lomas' claim pending the agreement, with the Land Office stamp of today's date on it.'

Henty nodded, and using a sheet of

headed paper wrote out the necessary screed and rubber-stamped it. Mark folded it and tucked it away, then the two men shook hands and parted company.

Rod Denning and the Dando brothers pulled up outside the HB ranch-house, and leaving Will and Henry to seek the shade of the verandah, Denning pushed through the door and waited for the sharp-eared Lo Sing to appear. The little Chinaman was at his elbow as though by magic. 'You want Boss Bowden?' he asked. 'I tell him you here. You wait.'

Denning scowled at the man's back. He didn't take kindly being told to wait, and when the order came from a yellow-faced heathen, it got his dander up. Henry Bowden's expression when he came through the inner door did nothing to ease his feelings. The man's face was as black as thunder.

'Now what in Hades has gone wrong?' he barked. 'You should be keeping Holden until the day after tomorrow.'

Rod Denning swallowed down the hasty reply that raced into his mind, he had too much at stake to fall foul of Bowden now. He shrugged his shoulders in a deprecating manner. 'That hombre was sure enough born under a lucky star,' Denning began, and Bowden snorted like one of his Lippizanas. 'We were trailing him nice and easy, knowing just where we'd take him when he headed up over the Divide, an' he knew just where he was heading, like he'd been brought up on the blamed mountain. We followed his trail easy enough, but 'way up in the snows it petered out where it seemed we had two chances, we followed the inside trail that was sheltered by the outer wall of the mountain, an' when it opened out we found it came to a stop at a glacier that was a few thousand feet long. Sam and Frank Dando found out the hard way; they were on the trail that broke from under 'em, an' right now they're piled up dead somewhere at the foot of the glacier. The outside trail ended up at the same place so where Holden lost us is anybody's guess. Anyways, there was no way Will and Henry Dando would go on. With two brothers killed, they'd had enough.'

Henry Bowden's steady gaze stayed on Denning's face as he thought things through, then he shrugged his wide shoulders. 'I guess there's no sense in crying over spilt milk. I'll settle Lomas' hash some other way. You'd better get that herd ready for rolling. Leave word when you're on your way. How many do you reckon you'll get through the pens?'

Only then did Bowden push a bottle and glass towards his ramrod. Denning filled his glass before answering; the thought flashing through his mind that his boss had made no mention of the two dead Dando brothers, and his own death would receive the same lack of concern, so his reply was given with added satisfaction. 'Somewhere just over three thousand I guess.'

Bowden nodded, a satisfied look on his face. 'The way things are just now, an' the way prices usually move I reckon you should get thirty-five dollars a head, anyway somewhere between thirty and forty. You're on a personal take of two dollars a head, separate from wages. Sooner you're back with the note, sooner you get paid.'

Denning drained his glass while Bowden was speaking, then he looked his boss in the eye and nodded equally. 'I'll let you know when I've got 'em on the move.' Then he rejoined the Dandos, his mind working on the pleasant sum that spelled out a life of comfort for him.

As the three men rode away from the HB, Denning told Will and Henry Bowden's instructions; neither man made any comment. The death of their brothers had affected them so that apathy had taken over. Denning realized they needed to fix the blame for their brothers' death on someone specific, so they could revenge them, and he reckoned he could point the blame squarely onto Holden. 'Let's head for the Crippled Wagon and get rid of the alkali then get ourselves some chow.'

Walt Maggs eyed Denning and the Dando

brothers with acute misgivings as they pushed their way into the Crippled Wagon. The youngster eased through the raised flap and pulled out chairs from under a table well within his earshot from the bar and waited for the men to come alongside, inferring that they were favoured customers. Denning halted his march to the bar and the grin that was always on his face widened as he took the seat Walt proffered. Will and Henry Dando sat down without a glance at the youngster.

'Bourbon,' Denning said. 'Make it a couple of bottles.' And as Maggs went to the bar he eyed the youngster, noting all the signs that pointed to growth into very rugged and active manhood. He thought that if Maggs already held him in high esteem, he could do worse than foster it. It wouldn't be too long before he'd be parting company with the Dando brothers, he could do worse than groom the youngster to stand at his shoulder.

When Walt returned with the bourbon and glasses Denning caught his eye. 'You like this job?' he asked.

Walt gave him a frank look and considered a little before replying. 'I guess I'm lucky to draw a man's wage, so like it or not I'd do my best to keep it.'

'What'd you say if you had the chance to earn a man's wage herding cattle?'

'I'm not free to make any choices, Mister Denning. I've got a mother an' youngsters to feed right here in Kremmling, an' that needs regular money.'

Rod Denning nodded. 'Yeah, I see the problem.' He shrugged his shoulders as though he had dismissed the matter, but as Walt Maggs took his place behind the counter, he determined to take the youngster on the drive, and school him in the job of being his shadow. It was as well that he could not read what lay behind Walt's beaming smile. In Maggs' book anyone with the taint of the mining company held a share in the responsibility for his father's death.

At the moment young Walt's concern was for Mark Holden, and he strained his hearing for any clues from the three men as to what had happened to him. The absence of Sam and Frank Dando suggested that somewhere they were keeping Holden prisoner. In between attending to the half-dozen other tables with their thirsty human flotsam he kept Denning and the Dando brothers under surveillance. He watched them dispose of the first bottle in silence, and although Denning's grin gave him the appearance of good humour, Will and Henry Dando looked totally apathetic. He found that surprising; he'd understand Sam and Frank being morose standing guard on Holden somewhere, but Will and Henry should be drinking with the enjoyment that went with good luck.

Everything became clear to him as he

117

passed close to their table to answer a call for a bottle from a table near the door. 'Don't seem right,' Will Dando was saying. 'Drinkin' here large as life, an' Frank an' Sam lying dead up in that goddam mountain.'

As he passed close again Denning was talking. 'Yeah, that hombre Holden knew he was being tailed. He led us by the nose to where the trail caved in. I had a hankering for salivating him myself, but I guess you two will want to settle his account to keep things square.'

'You're durned right!' Will Dando snarled. 'So drive or no drive I'm gonna be here in two days when by my reckoning he should hit town.'

'Yeah, that goes for me too,' Henry growled without looking up.

Denning nodded and leaning over spoke quietly, but Walt Maggs' sharp ears picked up enough. 'You two can bring in the supply wagons an' pick up the stores for the drive, the day after tomorrow, so you'll have the day to pick your best chance. I'll be fetchin' in the beeves outa Long Valley ready to mix with the herd at the north trail from the Anvil.' He drained his glass before easing back the chair and standing up. 'Let's get outside some chow.'

The Dando brothers gulped down what remained in their glasses and followed Denning without a word, while at the bar, Walt

118

Maggs seethed with excitement and had difficulty in containing himself until his relief took over a couple of hours later. He was cagey enough to take a devious route to the stage-line stables to pass on the information to Joe Hollins.

'That's welcome news, Walt,' Joe was saying, when the noise out front heralded the arrival of the stage from Granby; just stay a while an' you can tell Miss Kate the same as you told me.'

The youngster shook his head. 'No, I don't want to be seen hanging about near the stage-line or they might be careful of what they say when I'm around. Rod Denning offered me a job today riding herd for man's wages, but I told him much as I'd like it, I had ma and the young 'uns to look after right here in town.'

By the time Walt had made his circuitous route to the small wooden house at the end of town, Joe Hollins was passing on the information to Kate Lomas, Dale Webb and Betsy Gray.

They all pitched in together to get the team cleaned, fed and bedded down and cleaned the coach before gathering in a group to consider things.

'Only one thing for it,' Kate said at length. 'You, Dale, and Betsy will have to do tomorrow's run. Doc Holden could turn up in town the day after tomorrow an' wouldn't know the Dando brothers were laying for him. I guess Joe and me will have to keep Will and Henry in sight and shoot 'em as soon as they get itchy fingers. If you get as much Indian cover as on these last two days then you'll have nothing to worry about. They sure enough wet-nursed us all the way.'

'You've no cause to worry on our account,' Betsy Gray said emphatically, 'Dale an' me'll handle anything that comes up.'

'You're durned right,' Webb added. 'And that's the sweetest team it's ever been my luck to handle.'

'What happened about those two hombres who bought tickets just when you were leaving?' Hollins asked.

'They didn't cause any trouble,' Kate answered. 'When I told 'em of the trouble we had on the last run they understood, and they understood better when we had the Indians riding close. If they'd had guns handy they'd have used 'em, and spoiled things. Anyway, they've booked to return day after tomorrow.'

Kate, Betsy and Dale Webb were about to leave when Hollins stayed them. 'I've been getting around the last couple of days,' he said, 'and a lot of folk are ready to follow a strong lead against the mining company. I've told 'em we'll be in touch with 'em as soon as Doc Holden wants to move.'

EIGHT

Mark Holden pulled Chief to a halt and surveyed the gimcrack entrance to Dave Lomas' mine. The board carrying the old-timer's name hung from one nail fastened to the crosspiece supporting timber, and the overall appearance suggested that the pursuit of riches in this particular hole in the ground would be foolhardy, that the only sure return from endeavour would be a bad back.

He had ridden in from the south, joining the route Lomas would have to take if the mining company kept the old road closed. He wasn't disposed to enter the workings, not having enough knowhow to be able to assess the value of the claim. He concluded however that if Bowden wanted it, then it must be worth the having. As he stared at the swinging sign his mind slid back to the part of his medical course that covered poisons, and he remembered that galena was high in the mineral list, and galena was lead ore. Mark slid to the ground and looked around, and sure enough he saw amongst the spoil, small grey, opaque cube-shaped stones. Picking a couple of them up he found that although they conformed to the cube shape, the edges were smooth, and already the reason for the death of young Indians seeking out the help of the Great Spirit was forming in his mind. He remembered his own time, when the only solace he was permitted was a pebble under the tongue. The smooth-edged cubes would have attracted any youngster starting his fast, and seeking his dream, and without any other liquid to flush the poison away the saliva would become lethal. He pocketed the cubes before climbing back into the saddle, with the intention in mind to see White Eagle to explain the deaths of the Indians on the mountain they called the Eagle of Death. Perhaps White Eagle would call a conference of chiefs and medicine men to get the taboo lifted from the mountain. Such action would place the mining company's activities in jeopardy.

When the trail joined the road from the company surface buildings to the Kremmling to Granby stage route, he took the left-hand turn, and the gradual slope to the busy, noisy scene that characterized deep-mining and the extraction of metal from the base rock. He gained level ground and saw that the totally enclosed furnace and running-shed were working. Smoke poured out from vents high in the side of the buildings, and he concluded that they were extracting silver.

The word must have been passed from

mouth to mouth, and he saw someone slip into the big wooden office, to return followed by Mayhew and three others. He eased Chief to a halt and waited for the mining boss to close the distance. Mayhew's face was as black as thunder and his three followers all carried scatter-guns. He came to a stop a few yards away from where Mark sat the big stallion nonchalantly.

'Last time you were here, Holden, I told you to fork your freight. I meant that permanently. So just turn around an' keep going. Look back an' these jaspers'll fill you full of buckshot.' Mayhew's eyes fairly glittered as he spoke.

'If you don't hear me out, Mayhew, you're gonna have a hole in your forehead, and a couple more of your sidekicks, too. Just mebbe, one of the three will get lucky.'

Mayhew stared hard at Mark, and the calm, and mockery of the doctor's expression held him. He motioned to the men alongside him to hold their fire, then spoke in icy tones. 'If you've got something to say, Holden, spill it, an' then get to heck out of it.'

'Just this, Mayhew. I've got a land registry letter stamped an' signed by Henty that says this road is a right of way for Dave Lomas and his assigns. And I can tell you that you've not had permission to buy the road. In fact the whole blamed mining company could be sent packing if pressure if put in the right quarters. This is Indian territory, the three mountains and Bowden's ranch, an' unless there's a lot of back-tracking in Kremmling, like giving back what's been stolen or taken at the end of a gun, then you've got a lot less time than you think.' As he spoke Mark saw Henry Bowden emerge from the silver furnace building and head in his direction, so he added quickly, 'Your boss is on his way, Mayhew, you'd better wise him up.'

Mayhew was the picture of malevolence as he turned to check for himself, then with a peremptory order to the other three men to keep their eyes on Mark, he moved off to meet Bowden half-way. The two men conferred then Mayhew turned away and headed for the silver furnace, and Bowden took his time in getting to where Mark waited in apparent calm.

Bowden appeared unruffled as he came up. He muttered a word to the men and they turned on their heels to go back towards the building they had vacated. He eyed Mark speculatively. 'It looks like you decided against taking my offer of being the Company doctor,' he said. Mark just nodded, then: 'I'd like to see that letter from Henty.'

Mark reached into his inside pocket, and handed the letter to Bowden who came close to reach it. Wordlessly, the mining company owner scanned it and handed it back. 'Well it don't make much difference,' he said calmly.

'By the time Lomas is fit to do any digging, the purchase will have gone through.'

Mark's laugh was short and derisive. 'Things are not going to be that easy for you, Bowden! I guess when I was dodging those five hombres you had trailing me I had time to think about things, an' I reckon I came up with the right answers after hearing about the hombre who ran that Assay office before Henty, and seeing the map of the territory.'

'You're talking in riddles, Holden! I had nobody following you.'

Mark shook his head. 'You set Denning and the Dando brothers on my trail, Bowden, and two of 'em are lying dead at the foot of a glacier somewhere up on the Divide. Somewhere in these buildings, too, you're nursing three hombres I slugged when they were chasing the stage the day I hit town. You knew too this is Indian territory, and the mountain is taboo to 'em, so you knew you'd be left alone long enough to be able to regularize things.'

Bowden's eyes were thoughtful as they held Mark's unwaveringly then, as he laughed sneeringly, 'It don't matter a hill of beans what you think, Holden. I told you last time we talked I can't be responsible for every hombre who works for the Company. I allow there's more'n one who's looking for a quick buck, and I guess they'd rob me as soon as anyone else. Sure I knew this is Indian territory, and that this particular mountain is taboo for 'em, but I pointed out to Henty that Tagget used an old map, an' that he'd better get things sorted out.'

'Y'know Bowden, I've got nothing against folk mining for lead an' silver, and if you did just that without trampling everyone underfoot, then I'd ride into the sun an' leave you to it, but before I leave Kremmling I'd need to see the Lone Star and the Anvil handed back to the men who were driven out by Denning's gunslingers, Rudge and his deputies sent packing, an' all the saloons and stores handed back to their rightful owners.'

Henry Bowden stared at Holden. 'You're loco, Holden, plain loco, an' it don't matter one way or another to me whether or not you ride into the sun or stay an' die of old age.'

Mark shrugged his shoulders. 'Well, I guess the talking's done.' He took time out to build himself a smoke, and when he had the cigarette alight, he turned the big stallion around, and rode a couple of hundred yards back-trail before turning off to his left, down the slope and across the stream. When he reached the point where he had last sent the smoke message to White Eagle he dismounted and started collecting brushwood. Bowden stood where Mark had left him, still fighting down an impulse to put a bullet into the doctor's back; he had caused plenty of men to die, but killing was for hirelings, that way he could always get out from under.

He was about to turn away to rejoin Mayhew and make plans for Holden's early death when the actions of the distant doctor held him. Holden was gathering brushwood and pulling out tufted roots of grass, making a pile of them, then the doctor took out a blanket from his saddle-roll. Bowden watched the fire start, and after a while smoke rise, then Holden take position beside the fire with the blanket to send puffs of smoke soaring aloft in differing intervals. For fully five minutes Bowden watched the message float skywards before disintegrating. When he saw Holden repack the blanket and climb into the saddle there was a niggling doubt in the company owner's mind.

Mark breasted the rise of the first foothill and headed down the steady gradient of the plateau towards the next steeply rising hill that was split by four canyons. He had been under surveillance, and no sooner had he topped the ridge than Cheyennes streamed out of the canyons and rode towards him with lances held high. Mark eased Chief to a halt to await the phalanx that flanked him each side, with shouts of welcome, leaving the way clear for White Eagle to ride through to greet him.

With his arm raised in salute, Mark looked slowly along each phalanx, catching the eyes of braves he had been brought up with, and every face carried a smile; then he slid to the ground, as did White Eagle, and they met, embracing each other in welcome.

After the first exchange of conversation Mark came straight to the point. 'Thank you for your warning about the five men who were trailing me, I was able to lead 'em into trouble and see to my affairs in Denver.'

White Eagle nodded. 'We saw three return and heard that two were dead at the bottom of "Slippery Foot".'

'Yeah,' Mark agreed. 'It was you who showed me the way through that cave entrance ten years ago; anyway, in the land registry office I found that the mountain, "The Eagle of Death", where the miners are digging for lead and silver, and the other two mountains and land between them an' these hills is all Indian territory.'

'That's right, Mark, but the "Eagle of Death" is taboo, and maybe soon the Great Spirit will kill those diggers the same as our people.'

Mark shook his head, and pulled from his pocket the cubes of galena he had taken from the mining area. He held them in his palm and held it out for White Eagle's attention. 'These are what killed our people.'

White Eagle looked at the two small

pebbles, then back at Mark before picking up the pebbles and subjecting them to much closer scrutiny, then at length said, 'So, Laughing Moose, tell me how.'

'Those pebbles are from the rock, galena, which bears the metal lead, and lead is a deadly poison if swallowed over a long time. Long before the white men came there were pieces of galena all over that mountain, and if left alone they wouldn't have killed any Indians.' White Eagle nodded, while a number of braves closed in, listening intently. 'We know that the only Indians who died on the mountain were those who had gone to pray to Wakanda, the Great Spirit, to have their dream and find their medicine. Well, we know that no matter how long it takes to speak to Wakanda, we take no food nor water, but to stop our tongues swelling and choking the life away we hold a pebble under the tongue. These pebbles poisoned the saliva. If other water was being drunk like at ordinary times, the poison wouldn't have been enough to kill, but, not being flushed out of the body the concentration of poison took the purity from the blood and destroyed the brain and other organs.'

White Eagle handed the pebbles to Flying Wolf. 'Before returning them to me, let them all see these, and remember them well, point them out wherever you see them to your squaws and papooses. They are taboo because Laughing Moose has told us so.'

The word was passed quickly, and each brave took time to memorize the colour and shape of the pebbles, and after a word from White Eagle to Flying Wolf, the latter despatched some braves who had seen the pebbles to keep watch at the ridge, then White Eagle and Mark sat down together and waited until they were joined by a half dozen minor chiefs before holding a pow-wow that went on for an hour and ended with complete agreement as to their future moves.

When Mark remounted Chief he waved his salute to his friends who, following White Eagle, sent their mounts racing for the four canyons. The sentries at the ridge waited for him to arrive, then one after another they rode up to him, touched his shoulder as he spoke each name, then lying low over their ponies hurried in pursuit of their fellows.

He reckoned he'd just about make Kremmling before the light failed.

Just an hour after sun-up the two lumbering supply wagons bearing the HB marking rolled up to the store situated a little downtown of the stage-office on the opposite side, where Harvey Brent did most of the graft for Luther Dill who had cheated him out of ownership at cards, with a fast gun to redress any accusation of cheating. Will and

Henry Dando climbed down from beside the drivers, and waited for four punchers to pull up behind the wagons, with the Dando brothers' cayuses in tow. They tied the animals to the hitchrail and went inside the stores.

Kate had finished her breakfast and was back in her bedroom when they stopped outside the store, and she hurried to the stables to let Joe Hollins know.

'We'll take it in turns to keep watch from the window,' Joe said, 'an' the other one can take a walk down Main Street an' back just in case they move around any. But I don't think we've gotta worry this side of mid-day. There's no way Mark can make it back by then.'

When she returned to her room it was to see Will and Henry emerge from the store and step out together towards the Crippled Wagon, then she saw Doctor Knowles on the other sidewalk, carrying his black leather bag, walking with short, confident strides. He didn't even glance across at the Crippled Wagon, but stepped down from the sidewalk directly opposite the stage-office and crossed the road. She smiled to herself at the first signs of his returning self-respect and hurried down to greet him.

Together they went in to see Dave Lomas, who was wide awake and definitely on the mend.

131

'How're you feeling this morning, Dave?' Knowles asked, placing his bag on the table beside the bed.

'A whole lot better'n I was, Doc,' Dave replied. 'I can move around a bit now with no more'n a twinge of pain. I reckon you'll have me to rights purty soon now. I guess I'd like to thank you for your attention.'

'Yeah, well maybe I've helped a bit, Dave, but for the most part you can thank young Holden.' He scowled a bit as he spoke. 'Just don't tell him I said so.' He let that admonition sink in then said briskly, 'Well, I'm gonna take a look and rebandage you, Dave, then I'm gonna make some calls on a few folk I've neglected longer than I like to think.'

'And when will you be in again, Doctor Knowles?' Kate asked.

'A couple of hours before sundown, I guess,' he replied.

'It's likely you'll be home then when Doctor Holden returns from Denver,' Kate said conversationally. There was a glint in her eye that didn't escape Doc Knowles, but he held his tongue. He knew he was finished with the horse-trough treatment, but he didn't want to talk about it.

Kate left them together and had a few words with Hannah Lord before taking her place at the window to check on the activity in the street. The punchers had started to load the HB wagons, but Will and Henry Dando were not in evidence. As she watched, Joe Hollins passed along the opposite sidewalk and walked between the wagons and the store, then crossing the street, seemed to Kate to be making for the Crippled Wagon. She noticed the Joe was wearing two guns, tied low, and she muttered a prayer that he wouldn't provoke anything. Hollins was a good enough marksman but he'd win no prizes going for the draw.

Joe, as Kate had guessed, pushed through the doors into the Crippled Wagon, immediately catching sight of Will and Henry Dando, seated in sprawling comfort at a table quite close to the bar. Two other tables were occupied by miners. Walt Maggs followed Joe approach, a half-smile of welcome on his lips.

'What can I get you, Mister Hollins?' Walt asked as Lomas' stableman reached the bar.

'Just one large slug o' rye, young feller,' Joe replied, 'enough to take the tang of leather-oil outa my gullet.'

'Now you know why I took this job when it was offered,' Walt said as he filled a glass; then when he leaned over to take the money he whispered, 'If you ain't around, and they start anything in here I'll get one of 'em for sure.'

Joe flashed the youngster a surprised look, and Walt patted his side before stepping back a bit so that Joe could see he was wearing a long, brown apron that enveloped his body down to his calves. Walt had a slip-knot tied on his left hand side, so in a split second he could have the apron drop to the floor and the .45 Colt in his right hand.

Hollins nodded, tossed down his drink, gagged a little as the rye scorched his chest, then left abruptly, taking no notice at all of the Dando brothers. He returned to the stage-office and climbed the stairs to knock at Kate's room, and when she called out 'Come in,' joined her at the window.

'Those two hombres are at the Crippled Wagon, an' the way they've spread 'emselves tells me they don't expect to see the Doc any sooner than we do.' Kate merely nodded, and Joe looked thoughtful before adding, 'If by chance Mark slides into the saloon on hitting town early, he'll have one gun at back of him. Young Walt is packing an iron, an' nobody's gonna beat him for speed when they're not expecting him to draw.'

A worried frown creased Kate's face.' His mother's had troubles enough, we've got to see that Mark doesn't go into the Crippled Wagon. One of us has got to be out on that street all the time.'

'Yeah, that's how I see it, but I'll be glad to see what those hombres do when they've loaded up.' He nodded down towards the wagons. 'Anyways, we can't be carrying a rifle down there all day, so whichever of us is in the street when Mark shows up'll have to do the best with six-guns.'

Kate nodded her agreement. 'I'm taking a walk now, Joe, if you'll take over here. You can use my Winchester.'

'Your Winchester will suit me fine.' He sat at the window seat, his eyes glued on the two wagons. When Kate called out to indicate she was ready to go he glanced at her, taking in the side-arms tied low, and felt no tremor of doubt. He judged her a match for most men with the hardware.

Near to mid-day, when Joe Hollins was again on duty at the window, the HB punchers completed the loading of the two wagons, and tied nosebags around the necks of their mounts at the rail then helped the drivers fix feeds for the two teams, before taking out packages of food from under the canopy of the first wagon and following each other into Hegatty's saloon, alongside the store. Half-an-hour later the men emerged, slipped off the nosebags and watered the animals at the nearest trough. The drivers used leather buckets to slake the thirst of their charges, then with Will and Henry cayuses tied back to the hitchrail the HB wagons started rolling, and the punchers swung into their saddles, quickly rounding the wagons to get clear of the dust.

Joe relaxed with a deep sigh. Will and Henry were depending upon the element of surprise. They'd miscalculated some Joe thought with a flood of pleasure. The surprise was going to be on the other foot.

Just after mid-day Will and Henry left the Crippled Wagon, and after cautious glances along the street, walked to Hannah Lord's eating house. They ate through a hefty meal without any apparent enjoyment, totally abstracted, as indeed they were. They missed Frank and Sam. Although totally evil, they had the tenderness of wild animals for their own. So Will and Henry brooded over the fate of their younger brothers. They paid for their meal and went out into the sunlight to walk the length of Main Street with hot, watchful eyes on everything that moved. Near the southern end of the street they turned into Danby's grubby little saloon and sat at the dust-covered window with brimming glasses of bourbon.

They day wore on with the Dandos restlessly making frequent excursions into the street, squinting first along the dusty road out of town before covering the length of Main Street, and always they returned to Danby's saloon at the end of the street. They took their next meal singly, and Kate and Joe were caught up in the Dandos mood. One or other of them had to be on the street all of the time, and always near enough on hand to be of assistance to Mark the moment he hit town. At the same time they had to keep out of sight of Will and Henry, in case the brothers started putting two and two together, then with Sheriff Rudge scratching himself in the sun in front of the hoosegow, there were odd moments Kate and Joe didn't have as clear a view of things as they'd like, and anxiety built up in them.

They had hurried meals in Hannah Lord's in turn, and it was Hannah who calmed Kate's fears. They sat together in the big kitchen with a couple of Chinese helpers pandering to their every requirement with un-Oriental smiles.

'It's good sense to be watchful, Kate,' Hannah said, after she had listened to Kate for a while, 'but it's my bet you've got nothing to worry about. Doc Holden is nobody's fool, and knowing that Sam and Frank Dando got killed he'll be expecting trouble when he hits town.'

Kate passed on Hannah's observation to Joe when they changed over, and for a time the tension went out of them, but by late afternoon they were keyed up again, not knowing what to expect then, with an hour to sundown, the stage came rolling in, to stop in a cloud of dust in front of the depot.

Sitting on top were the two men who had just caught the stage out of Kremmling three days earlier. They were both in smiling good humour and held rifles, and beside Dale Webb, Betsy Gray sat relaxed and contented.

Dale Webb jumped to the ground, and opening the stage-door, stood aside while five passengers alighted, all miners, bound for Bowden's lead mountain. Dale started to climb up top for the luggage, but one of the men on the roof waved him away, then as Dale stood down the two men handed the luggage down to him. Kate came alongside as they dropped nimbly to the ground.

They took stock of each other, the two men tipping their hats politely while Kate smiled a welcome. She eyed the rifles in their hands, then the smile turned into a grin as she said, 'Well you said you'd be coming back, but I didn't reckon on having to pay you shotgun rates for coming.'

They laughed, and the older man replied in a Texan drawl, 'There'll be no charge, Ma'am. We just didn't feel right sitting comfortable when that purty young lady was gettin' shaken around on top.' He glanced significantly at the guns tied low on Kate's thighs. 'You're dressed kinda warlike for town. If you've got troubles coming up, then mebbe you'll tell us. It might help you to make up your mind if I order two seats on tomorrow's stage, one for me an' one for my prisoner. Incidentally it looked like your redskin friends were looking out for you everywhere that mattered.'

Kate made her mind up as she looked around the street to see Will Dando eyeing the group from further along the sidewalk, and Henry on the other side, walking slowly towards the south trail. 'Yeah, there could be trouble,' she replied flatly. 'If you'll come inside, we'll tell you about it.'

NINE

'I've gotta feeling, old fella, that we've got to travel easy into town.'

Mark's words were directed at Chief, but he was really thinking aloud. The stallion's ears pricked to prove he was listening, but the animal's senses were moving more on the lines of a good feed and warm stabling. They were a mile from town, and Mark's mind was actively working on what to expect. He knew that Denning was due to gather in cattle for a drive, but he couldn't see the Dando brothers leaving the territory without first having tried getting even for the death of their brothers. They had set out in pursuit of Mark Holden and it was Mark Holden they were going to blame for decimating their family.

He checked his side-guns, returning them to their holsters, and for a moment toyed with the idea of waiting for darkness and circling town to arrive from the northern trail, but he dismissed it. Better now, when he was attuned to the fading light, and anyone needing to be sure of his identity having to be in the open, and fairly close, before starting anything. Will and Henry Dando would believe they had the element of surprise, but Mark was ready for them.

Edging Chief onto the trail after his cross-country ride he was no more than two hundred yards away from Main Street, and the shadows were closing. When one hundred yards away he saw a figure move in the doorway of Danby's saloon; then slink back. The split-second impression was one of the black-bearded Dando brothers. He saw nothing move on the other side of the street, so Mark reckoned if he were right in his premise, the other brother was further downtown.

Slowly, Mark eased a gun into his right hand and humped a little in the saddle as though too tired to be watchful. The figure edged out from the doorway again briefly, and Mark knew the next time the man would be toting a gun. He was just ten yards away when the man stepped out into the shadows, with gun raised, and Mark fired. Then, as the man staggered and pitched to the sidewalk two more shots rang out. One crashed through the window of Danby's saloon where Dando had stood, the other must have lodged in the man who tottered out of a doorway on the opposite side of the street. As Mark slid to the ground two men stepped out from doorways further down the street, one each side, and made their way along the sidewalks, their gazes directed at the men lying inert, both held guns. Then men started vacating the saloons and gambling dens, first carefully, then later in a tumbling crowd.

Mark gained the sidewalk as the man turned over Will Dando's body, before turning to look at him. Both smiled at the memory of their last encounter. 'My moniker's Judah Swale, US Marshal Swale, an' my pard's Deputy Marshal, Hubert Wells.'

The latter was crossing the street, having satisfied himself that Henry Dando was as dead as his brother, and the crowd was getting bolder, closing the distance. 'We've been talking to Miss Kate,' Judah Swale said quietly to Mark, 'she told us these two hombres were laying for you.'

They gripped hands, and as Hubert Wells climbed up to the sidewalk he took Mark's hand in a firm grip. At the same time there was a shout from the other side of the street, and Henry Dando's name was bandied about. A couple of oldsters eased themselves around Mark and after gazing down at the corpse, gabbled away Will Dando's name as they moved back amongst the crowd.

'I guess you got that hombre,' Wells said to Mark. 'He was on his way down when I fired. My shot broke that blamed window; you're either faster'n greased lightning, or was expecting trouble.'

Before Mark could reply there was a lot of movement in the crowd, and Sheriff Rudge burst through, followed by four deputies.

Rudge took in the picture at first glance. Recognizing the big, bay stallion, he looked for Holden's body beside the horse, and cursed inwardly when his view took in Holden alive and well on the sidewalk talking to those hombres he'd told to leave town three or four days ago. His glance switched to the cadaver, and swore again. He had rushed out of the saloon with the sole intention of giving Will or Henry Dando self-defence clearance. During the day Will had told him they intended salivating Holden and he'd need to be on the street muy pronto to clear them.

Rudge got close enough to the sidewalk to see it was Will Dando who lay with the red stain on his chest, then his cold eyes swept over the three other men. He stabbed a forefinger at Swale and Wells in turn. 'I told you cardsharps to get outa town! Well, I'll tell you again, an' if you're not gone by sun-up you'll hang alongside Holden for killing the Dandos.'

'Ain't you going to investigate what happened, Sheriff?' Swale asked quietly.

'There ain't nothing to investigate!' Rudge snapped. 'Holden has killed before, he's too free with the hardware, an' the sooner we stretch his goldarned neck the better for this town.'

'This hombre was gunning for the young fella, laying in wait in that doorway,' Hubert Wells said, stirring Will Dando's corpse with his foot, 'an' his brother was waiting with a gun in his hand across the street. He stepped out with his gun aimed, but even then this young fella beat him to it. My pardner took out the brother when he showed himself with gun at the ready. Their irons are on the sidewalks.' Wells had spoken loud enough to reach the encroaching crowd, and the word was being passed back.

Rudge had trouble mastering his expression. The evidence was there for all to see, and a lot of folk now taking in the evidence had suffered at the hands of the Dando brothers. He turned his attention to Mark, who stood partly concealed behind Swale. 'Well, you can spend the night in the hoosegow, Holden, while I look into things. Hand over the hardware!'

Mark moved away from behind Swale and the gun in his left hand was revealed, rock steady, aimed at Rudge's midriff. When he spoke it was in level, cool tones. 'The only hardware you get from me, Rudge, is the first slug out of this gun. You're no more a sheriff than any renegade, for my money you're in the pocket of the mining company and the jackals who've cheated the folk of Kremmling out of what's theirs.'

There was a long period of silence when Sheriff Rudge hoped for action from one of his deputies, and weighed his own chances against Holden if such a diversion came.

145

During this time Holden's words had been passed along from Kremmling folk in the front of the crowd, and what started as a murmur rose in a crescendo of noise as the townspeople rallied to Mark's side, and cries of 'Rudge out!' were raised. Joe Hollins' words around the town were bearing fruit, and suddenly, it was no contest as the four deputies found four .45 muzzles stuck into their backs, held by Joe Hollins and Kate Lomas, who had worked their ways through the crowd.

'Drop that belt of yours, Rudge! And head for the gaolhouse!' Mark ordered. 'Unless you want to be gathered up same time as the Dandos.'

Blind fury welled up in Rudge. Hate and need for revenge pounded his mind. He'd had things so nicely sewn up in Kremmling that his bankroll piled up without effort, and now, this callow, young doctor stood in his way. As the mists cleared from his eyes, so his belief in his prowess with the gun came surging back. He was still sheriff, and if he outgunned Holden then no-one else would horn in. If he killed Holden, then his life was still just round the corner.

Rudge's nerve-ends tingled as he made up his mind. He felt the blood-lust run through him, and elation take over. Even as he schooled himself for the act he moved his hands slowly around the front as though to unfasten his gunbelt. Then with lightening speed he went for his guns.

In that aeon of time Mark discarded his advantage of the gun in his left hand, and as Rudge's hands blurred from the front, he grabbed for his right-hand gun. They cleared together and three shots were fired, the explosions merged to sound as one. A few seconds ticked by before it was clear to any onlooker who had won, then the two guns dropped from the nerveless hands of the sheriff before he pitched face-down into the dust. The bullets from his guns had chipped away pieces of the sidewalk.

Judah Swale looked at Mark, and remarked with some asperity in his voice, 'I'd say you'd taken fair play beyond the range of common-sense. You didn't ought to give polecats like Rudge any chance at all. You should've used the gun you had ranged on him.'

Hubert Wells stepped down from the sidewalk and stood facing the four deputies for a minute, studying each man in turn. Then he barked, 'Unhitch those belts and let 'em drop!' They did so immediately, releasing Kate and Joe Hollins to move forward to greet Mark. Then he said deliberately, 'Until a new sheriff's elected I'll be doing the job. None of you hombres are needed, so hightail outa town before I dig back far enough for a reason to keep you here, under lock and key.'

The four men turned and pushed their way

through the now hostile crowd, only stopping to gather their possessions together before making for the stables.

Eager hands carted away the mortal remains of the three dead men to the funeral parlour, and Mark, now astride Chief, with Hollins, Kate and the two newcomers made their way to the stage-office.

Later, cleared of dust, and fed, they gathered together and Mark told them of the deaths of Frank and Sam Dando, and what he had discovered at the land registry office. Judah Swale told them of his and Hubert Wells' interest in the town of Kremmling.

'Three months ago, Ron Haskins who runs the Cross Keys outfit down at Sweetwater, called into headquarters in Austin to report he'd seen a bunch of killers in Denver. He had been passing through after visiting a sister in Medicine Bow, Wyoming. They were the same hombres who about five years ago had left him for dead about fifty miles out of Houston, alongside the Brazos River. He had seen the men before at Galveston with a herd of cattle that was being lifted out of the sea into a boat off Galveston Island. There was another small herd to be boarded before the Cross Keys beef was due to be ferried out to a deep-water vessel, and Haskins had moved around the shipping point a lot so he had every last one of that outfit clear in his mind.'

Swale paused to light a cigarette before continuing. 'About twenty miles out of Houston the Cross Keys men came across the bodies of the four men whose herd had been loaded immediately before their own steers. They had all been shot from behind, and the only thing the Haskins brothers found on the bodies was a receipt for seven hundred and fifty steers from the Hammer Ranch, Cameron, Texas. The next morning, near mid-day, coming to the end of a canyon, and remembering the way the Hammer men had been gunned down, the Cross Keys crew of ten men stopped and Ron Haskins climbed up one side of the canyon wall to get a view of what lay beyond. Anyway he had made half-way when he heard a shot and immediately lost consciousness.' Judah Swale relit the cigarette that had gone out in a slow, deliberate manner, conscious of the eager interest displayed on the faces of his listeners.

'Well! Come on, Mister Swale, tell us the rest,' Betsy Gray broke in. She couldn't sustain suspense for too long.

Slade smiled, then continued, 'Haskins must have regained consciousness in a few minutes. He was lying across a slab of rock, with a clear view of the canyon floor. Blood had run from a wound at the top of his head all over the side of his face, and he realized that viewed from the ground he would appear dead. Down below he saw men sprawled in death, and moving around them, going through their pockets, were the ten men he had seen at Galveston.

'They stopped searching when one man pulled out a receipt from Des Haskins' pocket before taking the saddlebag from the mount Haskins had ridden. The man opened it up and called the others saying, "We've got what we want, let's get rolling." Then the men drove the horses out of the canyon and Ron heard them ride away from beyond the canyon a few minutes later.

'It took him a long time to bury his two brothers and the other seven men under piles of stones before walking out of the canyon and looked for the horses the gang had driven away along with the cavvy. He had his horse trained to come at a whistle and sure enough it did. When he headed for Sweetwater he had collected six other horses. Until he was just a few miles south of Lampasas he had those hombres' trail clear in front of him, and he came to a small ranch where there were three dead men in the compound, one in the bunkhouse, one just inside the door of the ranch-house, and there were four women, two young and two old ones, with their clothes ripped from them and bullet wounds in their stomachs. There was nothing he could do except report it all in Lampasas. Their trail had moved east and he was headed north-west. Well, to come to the end of it, Ron Haskins trailed 'em back from Denver to Kremmling, and stayed long enough to find out who they were. The sheriff, Rudge, was one of 'em, so he decided to pass it all to us at Austin. The bossman was riding a big, white stallion, a breed he'd never seen before.'

A full minute went by as the others took in the story of brutal murders and worse meted out by men who had mixed amongst them in Kremmling during the last three years. Only then did Kate break the silence.

'You said you were taking tomorrow's stage with a prisoner, Mister Swale. Who's the prisoner?'

Judah Swale gave a wry grin. 'I guess I'm cancelling that booking, Miss Kate. I would have been taking Rudge to the hoosegow in Denver. I guess the Doc has cut down our chore by half, having already accounted for five of the hombres Haskins named. I'm hoping though to take the others back alive to answer for all their crimes, but more particular for what they did to the women near Lampasas.'

As they were considering Swale's words Joe Hollins left for the stables. It was the time that Walt Maggs got relieved from duty, and sure enough Joe had barely entered the stables than Walt arrived. It took only a few minutes for Walt to pass on what he knew, and for Joe to tell him what had taken place out in the street and what was taking place inside the stage-office rooms. They parted company for Walt to get home without being seen and Joe to return to the meeting. He was on time to get a slug of rye, and for Mark to pose him a direct question.

'You've been asking around town, Joe, for folk who're good and ready to make a stand against the mining company; how've you figured out?'

Joe took a deep draught while he got his thoughts in order, then replied with some enthusiasm, 'Better'n I thought it'd be, Mark. Since you've started standing up to Bowden's gunslingers there's a lot ready to back your play; folk like Hank Dean and Lew Tome who ran the Lone Star and the Anvil, Mulcahey of the Crippled Wagon, Henry Brent who owned the store before he got cheated out of it by Luther Dill. They reckon they can get together a following and stand a good chance of taking a grip on the town, but they're not so sure they can handle the miners if they come all in a bunch. One thing more, young Walt Maggs heard Will and Henry Dando talking about how Denning intends taking to the pens a couple of thousand head more than Bowden knew about, with the take to be shared three ways.'

'Young Walt is sure worth his salt,' Mark remarked, 'and I hope the townsfolk of Kremmling remember him if they get the place back to themselves.' There were grunts of approval, then Mark continued, 'I guess if things go according to what I've planned, then in five or six days the mining company'll fold up, and Marshal Swale and Deputy Marshal Wells will have done their job. It depends a lot on what friends of mine are doing in the mountains, and until I say the word I don't want anybody in town starting anything. When I want 'em it will be for one ride only, and that won't be to the Company's workings.'

Joe Hollins nodded his head, then stood up. 'Well if I'm gonna get the stage ready for tomorrow I've got plenty of chores to see to.'

The others looked at each other and agreement was reached without a word. They all trooped out behind Joe, and it took only half-an-hour to have the coach spick and span and all of the horses spruced up and comfortable for the night.

Ezra Cummings was in the crowd and saw Sheriff Rudge outgunned by the young doctor. He had been in Angie's dance-hall when the shooting had started and was in the forefront of the crowd when the names of the victims on the sidewalks had been shouted around. Two days earlier, when he and Rod Denning had exchanged a few words, he had been told of the deaths of Frank and Sam Dando. So now all the Dandos were dead.

For a long time Cummings had been Denning's eyes and ears in Kremmling, and nothing of consequence happened likely to affect Denning's interests there without Ezra Cummings putting him wise. In the days when Denning had gone in for straightforward robbery and killing, Cummings' spadework had been worth a lot more than the riders who took active part.

So it was about three hours later that Cummings tied his mount to the hitchrail in front of the Anvil. The ranch-house had run down considerably since the last of Lew Tome's hands had been sent packing, and the rancher forced to accept a dollar a head for the beef scattered on his range. Even at that price he'd been cheated, as many Anvil cows had been hazed off into Long Valley to serve the dual purpose of escaping the count, and providing Denning with a copper-bottom nestegg should he ever all out with Bowden.

The big room inside the double doorway was comfortable enough, and the range of drinks sitting on a side table was good enough to satisfy most men. Cummings went from room to room but finding no-one around he settled in a chair close to the drinks, and when he had half emptied a bottle of Old Crow he sunk further in the chair and slept.

He awoke later at Denning's voice saying, 'Howdy, Ezra. What brings you here so late?'

Cummings struggled up straight in the chair and grinned at Denning, who had turned up the big oil-lamp. The grin faded as he remembered the reason for his visit. In the meantime Rod Denning filled a couple of glasses with Old Crow and, after handing one to Ezra, pulled a chair close and sat down.

'Things have been happening in town, Rod, since you were there a couple of days ago.' He paused to take a drink.

Denning smiled. 'I was relying on just that, Ezra. You're gonna tell me that Will and Henry have salivated Holden, an' they're celebrating in the Crippled Wagon.'

Cummings gave his boss a long look, then shook his head. 'Nope, it didn't work out that way, Rod. They bungled it, Holden salivated Will, an' one of the two gamblers who had been in town a couple of days back, and came in again on today's stage, settled Henry's account. Then, to make it worse, Rudge talked himself into trying his speed against Holden. I guess he ended just as dead as Will and Henry.'

Denning said nothing for a long time. With the Dando brothers gone, and the protection of a crooked sheriff gone, and a hell-raiser like Doc Holden on a winning streak, Kremmling was beginning to look like a place to leave. His course of action stood out clear like the Pole Star in a black sky. His perpetual grin widened and Cummings, watching him, knew he'd made up his mind.

'Well, Ezra. I guess there's nothing to hold us here any longer. Maybe if we stayed and helped out then the Company might still win through, but we've got our reward right here. All we've got to do is get this herd we're collecting through the pens and we'll have all the dinero we'll need.'

Ezra Cummings' smile matched Denning's as the ramrod's assessment of things pointed in the direction he liked, then misgivings followed as Denning continued. 'Tell me, Ezra, would it concern Holden much if Kate Lomas went missing?'

Cummings looked at him levelly. 'Yeah, I reckon it would,' he said simply, and drained his glass as Denning made up his mind.

'Well, Ezra, this is the way of things. Next Wednesday I want this herd on the hoof, an' with the Dandos gone I'll need another four hands for the trail. Can you find that many you can trust now in Kremmling?' When Cummings nodded, he went on, 'Well, try grabbing Kate Lomas on Tuesday, get her to Long Valley, an' after we've tamed her some an' taken what Holden wants, we can throw her into the river that runs beside the valley; it runs fast enough to take her body clear to the Colorado, an' nobody'll be any the wiser.'

The little man's eyes gleamed with pleasure. Sensual to the last degree he liked best taking what was given under duress. A woman's distress merely heightened his pleasure, and he was already toying with the intention of taking her before delivering her into Rod Denning's keeping. He managed to hide his thoughts and listened for the ramrod's next instruction.

'One other thing. That young hombre, Walt Maggs, who's taken over as one of the barkeeps in the Crippled Wagon, I reckon he's made of the stuff we'll need to pack a gun for us. I sounded him out and he'd sooner earn a man's wage on the range than be a barkeep, but he's got a mother and family to look out for, so he's gotta keep the dinero coming. Tell him if he wants to come on the drive he'll get paid before we leave, an' we'll fix him up with a horse and gear before he leaves town. Give him a couple of days to make up his mind.'

'It'll be a long time before he'll be packing a gun that'll put him in the right class for us,' Cummings said quickly.

'Nope, you're wrong there, Ezra. When I spoke to him I could see the marks on his breeks where holsters had been strapped tight, low down. For my money that young hombre can throw lead with the best right now.' Rod Denning stood up as he spoke, and tossed off the remainder of his drink.

'Well I'm ready for some shut-eye. I'll see you before you leave in the morning. You know where to find the chow if you want it.'

'Yeah, I know. I'll mebbe have me a couple more slugs of Old Crow and doss down right here.' Cummings poured himself another glass as Denning left the room.

TEN

With the stage ready to leave for Granby the next morning an hour after sun-up, Judah Swale and Hubert Wells joined Kate Lomas, Doc Holden and Joe Hollins outside the stage-line office. Dale Webb gathered up the reins in high spirits, happy to have Betsy Gray perched on top riding shotgun. As Dale shook up the reins and gave the team a yell of encouragement old Dave Lomas appeared at the door of the depot. When Kate turned and saw him, he was shaking his head in sorrow.

'I sure hope they don't hit trouble,' he growled. 'That lass looks too purty to be riding shotgun an' mebbe shootin' for keeps.'

Joe Hollins turned around sharply, surprised to see Lomas. 'I guess most folk would say the same of Kate, Dave.'

'What are you doing down here anyway?' Kate asked. 'Did Doctor Knowles say you could get up from your bed?'

Old Lomas snarled. 'Yeah, he said I could try it out for a couple hours. I'm not going to take any chances; he said if I do myself any damage he'll go back on the bottle, an' take his chance with the horse-trough.'

Hollins and Kate laughed and looked at Mark who shrugged and grinned. Swale and Wells looked puzzled so Kate told them about Mark's efforts to encourage Doctor Knowles to take his drinks less often and in smaller quantities. Lomas failed to join in with the laughter, he had noticed Hannah Lord striding along the sidewalk preceded by two Chinese helpers, bearing dishes, and muttering to himself, he moved inside and up to his room. Kate joined Hannah and the rest went about their business, Mark to saddle up Chief and scout the range, Joe Hollins to move around town to talk to anyone he could trust about taking the town back from the Company stranglehold, and Judah Swale and Hubert Wells to take closer looks at the men in town they intended arresting when it suited them.

Hannah Lord didn't beat about the bush with old Dave. 'What in heck are you doin' out of bed, you old fool?' she yelled at him, as she pushed into the room. 'You ain't ready yet to get on yore feet. Anybody'd think you didn't want to get well an' settle down with a good woman.'

'Who in heck said I wanted to?' Dave growled, giving her a sharp look from under shaggy eyebrows.

'You did, when you were moaning in that bed like you were dying, an' more than once, in front of witnesses.'

'Whatever I said was only to get myself some peace, an' so's you'd go away.'

'Well, you ain't driving that stage again, no matter what,' Hannah said, a different quality in her voice. 'Now come an' get yore breakfast at the table, an' I'll sit up with you a couple of hours before getting you settled back in bed.'

'You've got no call to waste yore time sitting around with me.' Dave's eyes wandered to the breakfast uncovered, setting his juices running, mellowing him somewhat. 'But I guess I'm mighty glad you're ready to waste your time in yore own way.'

Kate looked in a few minutes later, and her father was managing very well one-handed, his eyes alight with appreciation of food, and Hannah, sipping coffee, was watching him with a tenderness that boded nothing but good for Dave. Kate felt happiness settle upon her. Changes were in the offing, things were about to happen, and she was glad that her father would be secure no matter what her future would be. He was immobilized, and so, out of danger.

Walt Maggs had been busier until mid-day than was normal. Throughout the morning townsfolk had been dropping in, mostly in pairs or small groups, taking tables well away from the bar, and whenever he got close to any of them they had clammed up. He felt there was something in the air, but his natural curiosity was left unsatisfied. Then when Ezra Cummings walked in, those men who were left sat back in their seats, seemingly interested only in their drinks. As Walt busied himself he found every time his glance settled on Cummings, the little man seemed to be studying him.

At length Ezra thumped his glass a couple of times on the table for a refill, and Walt took over the bottle of Old Crow that the man favoured. He smiled as he poured the liquid, and as he was about to turn away Cummings said, 'Hold on young fella.' Walt stopped and waited.

'I've been asked to pass on some information to you, an' to get your answer.' Then, when Walt turned full on to him and said nothing. 'Rod Denning told me he spoke to you about changing your job; seems he's taken a shine to you, an' I'll tell you for nothing, folk in Rod's good books do pretty well for 'emselves.'

Walt's thoughts slid away to the Dando brothers, they hadn't done too well, but his expression didn't slip. 'Yeah, but like I told him, I've got to stay here on account it's my money that keeps my family going.'

Ezra Cummings nodded, understanding in his eyes. 'Rod's idea is he pays you in full for the drive, that is wages only, before it starts, so your family will be taken care of

162

until you get back with bonus pay adding up to more'n you'd earn here in a year. He'd set you up with the best cayuse the livery's got an' all the gear you need.'

Walt's face mirrored his surprise, and Cummings went on, 'The drive for the pens starts Wednesday. He wants you to think it over an' let me know your answer tomorrow. If you want to take him up on it, then he'll want you at the Anvil Monday, a couple of hours after sun-up. I'd help you make your choice of cayuse an' gear an' ride with you to the Anvil.' He stood up and placed some coins on the table. 'He'll pay you for the drive on Tuesday so's you can see your folks before leaving and pass on the dinero to your mother.'

'How come he wants me that bad?' Walt asked, and Ezra Cummings pushed his Stetson to the back of his head and scratched, an expression of perplexity on his face.

'Right now I can't tell, but it could be he opines you've got class. He likes good company around him. I guess he's already noticed you're not afraid of work.'

With that Ezra Cummings turned and stalked out of the saloon, leaving a bemused Walt Maggs to ponder on Denning's offer. He had no way of knowing that Denning's sharp eyes had plumbed his secret ability with the six-guns. Walt gave it up; he'd pass the problem on to Joe Hollins just as soon as he was relieved to go home for his dinner.

Mark Holden worked his way through the mountains with all the cunning and craft of the Cheyenne Indians he had lived with for so long. He could picture the map he had studied with Henty in Denver, and was fairly sure that the Long Valley where Denning had the steers stashed that were to be included in the drive, lay north-west of the Anvil range, and he wanted to get the lay of the land so that he could lead the men raised in Kremmling to the right place during the early hours of darkness on the day of the drive.

As he guided Chief closer to where the valley lay, he was aware of the absence of Indians in these craggy foothills. He had seen a few sentries in the distance on the ridges that overlooked Bowden's HB ranch and the Company's workings, but it seemed that White Eagle had taken his main force deep into the mountains to confer with his father, Running Wolf, and the chiefs of the Sioux, Blackfoot and Crow. Still, the smoke signals would have sent the information ahead of White Eagle at almost the speed of the telegraph, and Mark had little doubt that they would believe his reasons for the deaths of the would-be braves on the Eagle of Death mountain, and he expected that when he met White Eagle on Monday, there

164

would be a sufficient number of Indians to do the chore he had in mind.

Unerringly he came upon the Long Valley, and by sheer luck at the only point that gave a clear view to the lush grassland far below. The width between the precipitous concave walls, sheer to the valley floor at this point would, he judged, give about three hours' direct sunlight to the grass below but the walls closed to a distance each side of his position where direct sunlight would be infinitely less. He saw the thin ribbon of fast-moving water running along the foot of the opposite wall. He also saw a couple of horsemen moving up valley with a bunch of cattle ahead of them.

Satisfied, he eased away from the edge and made his way as near parallel to the lip of the valley wall as the terrain allowed. It took him a couple of hours to reach the point where the foothills tapered down to merge with the rolling prairie below, but the curve of the valley went further north-west. He studied the surrounding country carefully for sign of riders, but there were none. Looking back towards the Anvil range he was able to pick out bunches of cattle, then to the east he noted the rolling foothills with a break opposite him where he guessed the trail herd would be driven through. He reckoned he was at the point where the cattle from Long Valley would be mingled with the Lone Star and Anvil stock.

Riding around the foot of the hill it took him an hour to come to the opening of a canyon where the walls almost met at the top. Pausing to check his guns, he urged Chief inside. If he was going to meet anyone in that canyon he opined he'd need to use them. He judged that the width of the entrance would permit three steers to travel together, and as his eyes became adjusted to the light as he moved in deeper, he saw plenty of evidence that shod horses used the canyon regularly. The entrance however had been swept clear of tracks by the use of blankets.

Luck was with him and he emerged at the head of the valley, where he saw in the distance large groups of cattle grazing contentedly. Cascading down the right-hand wall from halfway up was a waterfall of considerable proportions that ran away swiftly, keeping tight to the cliff wall. Turning Chief around he rode quickly out of the canyon. At the entrance he removed signs of his passage, then rode back to Kremmling by a route he intended to take with the men Hollins would raise to stop Denning's trail herd.

On the Saturday at mid-day Ezra Cummings sought out Walt Maggs in the Crippled Wagon. He wasted no time at a table, but took a glass of Old Crow at the long counter and waited for Walt to get a respite from his duties. 'Well, made your mind up, young fella?' Cummings asked, when Walt came to rest in front of him.

'Yeah, I guess so,' Walt answered quickly, his eyes gleaming with excitement. 'It's a chance I can't pass up. Just so long as I get the dinero to my mother before I leave on the drive.'

Cummings nodded. 'I reckon you're as smart as you look. We'll ride out to the Anvil Monday morning afore sun-up.'

'Just one thing,' Walt said slowly, 'I reckon Mister Sloan's gonna be all-fired mad at me turning this job in just when I'm getting the hang of things.'

Cummings gave a short laugh. 'Leave that problem to me,' he said easily. Pausing only to drain his glass, he lifted up the counter-flap and crossing to Sloan's office pushed the door open and walked through.

As Walt Maggs waited for Cummings to return, he was going over what Hollins had told him last night. 'Doc Holden wants you to take up Denning's offer. You've helped us to all the information he wants and here's your chance to get something back from what your family has lost. Get fitted up with a cayuse and all the gear. Get your pay for the drive, and when you ride back in on Tuesday night, stay at home. Denning won't be able to come looking for you. Just remember, act like you'll follow him anywhere.'

The excitement was building up in Walt. He had never owned a cayuse, the best he had done was ride bare-backed some of the livery horses around the big paddock, and the thought of owning one of his own with all the equipment, set his nerve ends tingling with anticipation. Ezra Cummings returned with Sloan just a couple of steps behind him, and Sloan's big hand clapped on Walt's shoulder.

'Now ain't you the lucky feller,' he growled. 'I guess I ain't the one to stand in the way of any hombre makin' good.' He turned to the till and withdrew a handful of coins which he placed in front of Walt. 'I reckon that'll pay for what you've done here. I'll look after things while you and Ezra pick up what you need, just come back an' work out the rest of the day; I'd have liked you to stay, but Ezra's fixed for someone to take your place.'

Walt scooped up the coins and looked Sloan in the eye, 'I'm more'n obliged to you, Mister Sloan. I'll be back just as soon as I can.' Then, turning to Cummings, 'I guess I'm ready just as soon as you want.'

Cummings glanced at Sloan, then led the way out of the Crippled Wagon, and Walt followed without a backward glance, excitement radiating his face.

On Monday morning long before sun-up, folk in Kremmling were on the move. One of the first was Dave Lomas. He was spruced up before Kate awoke, and when she emerged he declared he was in no pain at all and intended taking his breakfast at Hannah Lord's. When she was about ready she heard Mark Holden moving around, and when she presented herself Mark had taken a look at Dave's wound and declared himself satisfied that it would stand up to moving around, so to Hannah's surprise they arrived together at her eating house. She looked from Doc Holden to Dave and back to Mark.

'Is he fit enough to be up and about this early in the day?'

'Yeah, he's coming on fine. Just so long as he gets to his bed whenever he feels tired or gets any pain.'

'Aw quit fussin'. Years ago I kept straight on riding with worse'n this,' Dave growled.

'Yeah, years ago,' Hannah replied pointedly. 'It's time you took care now an' let a woman make a fuss of you.'

Dave pretended he hadn't heard and headed into the kitchen, but it was noticeable as he tucked into his breakfast that on the few times he glanced at Hannah his expression softened considerably.

They had almost finished breakfast when Dale Webb and Betsy joined them, both looking as though the day held nothing but pleasure for them instead of a gruelling drive to Granby. Betsy, bubbling with good humour and Dave hanging on to her every word. Dave, having now had proof of Betsy's ability to ride shotgun, was ready to lap up the good humour, and when Doc Holden and Kate left to help Joe Hollins get the stage ready, he stayed on to enjoy their company and bask in Hannah's close attention.

Joe Hollins was putting the gloss on one of the team leaders as Mark and Kate entered the stables, and when they picked on the next horses to be done, he said, 'I've just checked the livery, an' Walt Maggs rode out with Ezra Cummings more'n an hour ago.'

Kate glanced at Mark. 'Well at least,' she said, 'whether or not Denning pays him the money for the drive, he's got himself a horse and all the gear.'

They carried on and completed their chore, and when Hollins climbed aboard to drive the stage out front Mark held on to Kate's arm as she made to go through to the office. She looked at him, a question in her eyes, her nerve ends tingling at the contact. 'In a couple of hours I'm riding to meet up with White Eagle. Would you like to come?'

The question showing in her eyes changed to excitement. 'Oh – yes please.' And the extra pressure Mark exerted on her arm as he responded to her pleasure added to her excitement. She felt the colour riding in her face.

'Let's go and see the stage away,' she

breathed, in an effort to bring herself under control, and Mark followed slowly, affected by the little incident as much as Kate.

Later, after a long ride during which they had settled into a companionable, easy partnership, they pulled up just over the ridge of a hill that flattened at the top to a plateau ending a couple of miles distant at another thousand foot rise to the next escarpment, and atop that ridge was where Mark intended to wait for White Eagle. He scanned the ridge and sure enough he picked out sentries who had already recognized him, and could afford to be careless of their movements. Even though they were an advance guard, White Eagle would not be too far away.

'C'mon,' he said, turning to Kate and pointing to the ridge. 'My blood-brothers, the Cheyenne, are over that ridge.' Nothing loth, Kate gigged her Palomino into action and they rode directly for the rising ground.

When they had just a couple of hundred yards to go to the top of the ridge, horsemen waited above them, sitting their mounts in relaxed manner. Gaining level ground Mark drew rein bringing Chief to a stop, then raised his arm in salute to the Cheyenne braves who were closing in. He saw in the distance tepees springing up like mushrooms, and all the usual activities that went into making camp. White Eagle had arrived on time. He subdued the feeling of optimism as he greeted Crazy Hawk who came alongside him and pointed towards the tepees before galloping off, followed by half-a-dozen of the braves, the others spread out along the skyline.

White Eagle stood in front of his tepee, watching their approach, and Kate was amazed at the greetings and salutes of the braves who gave them a clear run to where their chief waited. Mark returned the greetings and Kate smiled doubtfully. When they dismounted a couple of braves led their mounts away, and taking hold of Kate's arm Mark led her to where White Eagle stood, his face impassive but a glint of interest in his eyes. The two men held arms and smiled at each other, then Mark said, 'My friend Kate Lomas; meet my blood-brother, Chief White Eagle of the Cheyenne.'

Kate held out her hand which White Eagle took soberly. 'Any friend of my brother is my friend,' he said in faultless English, 'especially a brave friend who rides guarding the stage-coach.'

Smilingly Kate replied, 'I'm pleased to be your friend, Chief White Eagle, and I guess Mark's lucky to have been raised with the Cheyenne.' The two men smiled, and Mark saw the question in his friend's eyes. Mark's expression inferred to his intuitive blood-brother that if things ran smoothly, Kate would be his woman.

They sat with other braves in a wide circle and ate a meal of pemmican helped down by water, and Kate was surprised both by their facility with English and the penchant for humour inherent in them all. She asked about the tepees, wondering at the speed they were erected, and White Eagle asked Crazy Hawk to show her how it was done, and with Kate out of the way, White Eagle came to the cause of the meeting.

'Running Wolf met the chiefs of the Sioux, Blackfoot, Crow and Ute and they agreed the pebbles caused the deaths on Eagle of Death Mountain. All the medicine men agreed that you would say nothing but the truth, so with the next but one sunrise there'll ten thousand braves on the mountain to claim it back from the miners.'

They clasped hands in complete accord and for the next half-an-hour Mark gave White Eagle a detailed information of his intended course of action, and the benefits he hoped would accrue to Kremmling and more important, to the Cheyenne. Eventually Mark stood up ready to leave, and Crazy Hawk brought Kate back while Walking Serpent collected their horses. White Eagle shook Kate's hand and a press of braves did the same smilingly. Mark and White Eagle clasped each other close, then Mark climbed into the saddle, turned full circle slowly, giving the Cheyenne salute, ending up facing White Eagle before easing Chief around and heading for the ridge. Kate drew alongside and Crazy Hawk raced past them, taking the lead with half-a-dozen braves riding each side of them. The sentries at the ridge signalled all was clear, and with Indian yells of encouragement in their ears Mark and Kate headed downhill towards the plateau of the next foothill.

Walt Maggs was feeling good, astride his own horse, a sturdy, young pinto mare, with two hundred dollars in his money belt and under instructions by Doc Holden to stay at home. He had nothing to worry about, he already had enough money to keep his mother and family for six months, and he felt sure that there would be no trouble finding work after the Doc had sorted things out in Kremmling.

He had spent two days under the tutelage of Rod Denning who had expressed pleased surprise at Walt's ability to draw and get close to a target, and Rod had gone on to show him all the skills he would be expected to master to pull his weight on a drive. It was some measure of satisfaction to Walt that when he left the Anvil, Denning had seemed happy at his progress; he was still wondering however why Denning had selected him to use on the drive.

When he guided his mount from the grass alongside the trail towards the mile-long canyon ahead, his mind was cleared of thoughts of Denning when a shrill succession of screams came from somewhere inside the canyon.

Walt slid out of the saddle and led the pinto to the side of the canyon mouth. There was nothing more he could do except wait. His sharp ears picked up the hoofbeats of two animals, and he palmed his right-hand gun, pressing back against the cliff side of the canyon entrance.

The hoofbeats sharpened and suddenly a rider whom he recognized as Ezra Cummings emerged, leading a laden packhorse with a slim, trussed figure tied across its back. Walt didn't hesitate. His first shot sent Ezra's Stetson flying, and when the startled man turned sharply in the saddle, dragging at his gun, Walt's next shot smashed into his shoulder, sending him crashing to the ground.

Kate was conscious and called out, bringing Walt immediately to her side. Checking that Cummings was in no fit state to constitute danger, he cut Kate adrift, and she regained her feet to rub the circulation back into her arms and legs. 'Well!' ejaculated Kate at length. 'I'm sure glad you happened along, Walt. It looked like my goose was cooked.'

'Nobody's more glad than me, Miss Kate. Just as well you screamed when you did or I'd have ridden right into trouble, I reckon he'd have been too good for me from a standing start.'

They checked on Cummings who was out cold, having hit a rock embedded in the trail, so, relieving him of his guns, they tied him on the packhorse, then with Kate astride Cummings' mount, she led the way back, with Walt feeling that things were going fine for him, bringing up the rear.

When the thin moon slid over the highest foothill to the east, Doc Holden's men were in position. Judah Swale and eighteen men were positioned east of the point where the cattle from Long Valley would be mingled with the Lone Star and Anvil stock, and Mark, Hubert Wells and a dozen more were well hidden with a good view of the entrance to Long Valley. They had a long wait but nobody minded. Today was when the decent folk of Kremmling were going to get even.

It was an hour and a half before sunrise that the distant bellowing of cattle told them the beef hidden in Long Valley was on the move. The first beast charged out of the entrance, a big, rangy steer with horns a foot longer than normal. He sniffed the air and looked around him, but there was only one way to go, so he turned right and lumbered off angrily. Two more came out tentatively, then three abreast, all turning to follow the lead steer, then cattle came spilling out at an even pace, controlled by the width of the near tunnel. The watchers lost count, and it took over half-an-hour for Long Valley to disgorge its cache of beef. Dust was emitted in clouds out of the narrow aperture between the cliff walls, and it was fully ten minutes before the riders came through the entrance, with hats pulled down over their eyes and bandannas over their mouths and nostrils. Rod Denning was first through followed by nine drovers.

Mark allowed them to travel a mile or so, then he passed the word to follow, just close enough to be on the spot when required, while remaining unseen.

Rod Denning was in a mixed frame of mind. His future interests now seemed assured with the herd on the hoof, but the long hours he had waited for Ezra Cummings to show up with Kate Lomas had gnawed at his very vitals. It still rankled that he had failed to strike at that blamed Holden where it hurt most. He even toyed with making a quick run into town to give the young doctor a fatal dose of Denning medicine, but he resisted the impulse as he caught up with the herd.

With the cattle moving at a steady pace

rounding the hill where the Anvil stock would join in, Denning was about to instruct his men to move around the flanks to bring the leaders to a halt, when all Hell broke out in front. Stabs of flame lit the night and a ragged succession of shots had the steers breaking away to his right, heading for the Anvil, and the increasing noise of steers raising their speed to stampede level drowned the noise of Mark's men bearing down from the rear. The whole herd had disappeared around the bend of the hill before Denning and his men turned in alarm to find determined horsemen almost on top of them. As they went for their guns, the men who had turned the herd from the front were shooting at them in earnest.

Blind hatred flooded through Denning as his carefully nurtured plans came apart. Instinctively he knew that Holden was at the back of things and with the determination to settle the account, he replaced his gun and slid to the ground, feigning death. By the time Mark's and Swale's men closed around the drovers, one man only sat immobile in the saddle with his hands aloft. The others lay where they had fallen. Swale rode alongside the man, looked closely at him, then shaking his head, took the man's guns, emptied the chambers and gave them back.

'You're lucky, hombre! Just ride out an' never come this way again!'

The man looked around at his fallen companions, and a big sigh escaped him. 'I sure appreciate it, mister,' he said. He turned his mount abruptly and headed north.

Denning squinted at the horsemen through slitted eyes, picking out Doc Holden who was studying the men on the ground for sight of him. The ramrod was halfway to his gun when Mark saw him and the two shots rang out together. Mark's slicker tugged at him as Denning's shot missed his heart by a fraction, while a short cry of agony escaped Denning as a bullet smashed into his wrist.

The dead men were tied over the saddles of their cayuses, and Mark attended to Denning's wound, before setting off in the wake of the Long Valley herd, Denning riding up front between Judah Swale and Hubert Wells. Mark, on the flank, led the whole string of horses bearing the corpses; with the arrival of dawn he wanted to advertise their success to the men the other side of the Lone Star and Anvil cattle. The ploy worked, and when the two herds mulled uncertainly, scouts from raised ground reported back to their confederates what they had seen, and when Mark and his men reached the herd, the drovers had ridden away, ostensibly to report back to Henry Bowden at the HB ranch. The herd was persuaded to move back towards the Anvil, then to the Lone Star before heading for the HB ranch which Bowden kept exclusively for his Lippizanas.

Dan Mayhew, the mining company's under-manager, woke up with his scalp crawling and nerve-ends tingling. He stared into the darkness, listening for the usual noises caused by a workforce preparing for the day's activities, but it was as silent as the grave. He sat up, reached for his clothes and dressed in the dark, then felt at the rail on the end of the bed for his gunbelt. Grasping it in the middle, it came up at him in a rush, and the significance hit Mayhew like a thunderbolt. In the darkness he crossed the floor of the hut and unerringly reached for his rifle, his blood chilled at finding it gone. He glanced through the window but it was only the shadow of the hut alongside that showed up.

There was nothing for it, he would have to find out what was amiss. Moving stealthily to the door, he turned the handle gently and drew it open. Tentatively he stared out then, seeing nothing, he stretched his head forward. Strong hands grasped and yanked him outside, then he was hauled to his feet, and tied expertly with leather thongs. His own bandanna was used to gag him before he was made to stand upright between two Indians who stood as tall as himself.

At last, with the first feint of dawn, Mayhew was led away to the open ground in front of the works buildings, and from every quarter the mine-workers in all states of undress were pushed along to stand in an ever-increasing crowd behind Mayhew. The light strengthened, and the captives found the entire mountain crawling with Indians – Cheyenne, Sioux, Blackfoot, Crow, Ute and a number of Mandans who had escaped the white man's plague.

With the dawn Henry Bowden stepped out-side to visit the big, white horses that were to form the nucleus of the school that would be his way into society back on the East Coast. He stopped stock-still, disbelieving the evidence of his eyes. The entire place was ringed by hundreds of Indians, all sit-ting impassively on their mounts, ominous and threatening; there were only four of his men around the place, all he could do was to affect pleasure at seeing them.

The ring of Indians moved inwards slowly. Two of his men came out of the Lippizanas' stable and the others came out of the ranch-house, to stop wholly transfixed then, when about twenty yards away, it was Crazy Hawk who gave an order to a brave alongside him. The brave wheeled and calling to a few men rode away. They returned with mounts for Bowden and the others, man-handling them onto the cayuses.

Astride the animal Henry Bowden looked around, and black rage shook him as he saw

Indians opening the wide stable-doors and the paddock gates and driving his Lippizanas out, and hazing them south. He and the other men were relieved of their weapons and about thirty braves closed around them to set them moving in the direction of the Eagle of Death Mountain.

Long before Denning's men got near to the HB ranch they became aware of vast hordes of Indians crowding the range, and they turned almost as one to take the quickest route to Kremmling and beyond.

Mark and his men had the herd moving easily and they were able to distribute the animals along the range, sharing them between the Anvil, Lone Star and then the HB before heading for the Eagle of Death Mountain. Indians crowded the ridges of the hills as they rode, and many lances were raised in salute as Mark raised his arm in acknowledgement. Swale, Wells and the Kremmling folk watched in utter amazement, then as a brave on the skyline moved his mount around in a few controlled movements to end up facing a direction in which he pointed his lance, Mark headed towards the mining company's workings.

'I've sure enough seen it all,' Judah Swale said so that a lot of other riders could hear, 'you're the first white man I've met who could raise an army of Indians at the drop of a hat.'

Mark grinned. 'It's not as simple as that. I only pointed out reasons for 'em to claim their territory back.'

When they arrived within sight of the workings a lot of the riders had nagging doubts. There were thousands of Indians in possession of Eagle of Death Mountain and Mark, sensing their disquiet, turned in the saddle, releasing the lead rein of the first horse bearing a corpse. He passed it to Hubert Wells. 'I guess you and the others had better stay right here. Then, to Judah Swale: 'If you'll come with me you can collect a couple of hombres you'll want to take in personally.'

Half-an-hour later they rode back down the hill and across the stream to rejoin Hubert Wells and the others, with two bemused prisoners riding between them. Dan Mayhew and Henry Bowden, officially charged by Judah Swale for the murders down on the Brazos, and the killings of men and women just out of Lampasas, were stunned at the change in their fortunes, and the sight of Denning's pain-wracked face and the line of corpses did nothing to help them; there'd be no rescue bid from that quarter. Their spirits sank lower every mile until they were at a very low ebb when the men of Kremmling rode on ahead to break the news.

There were crowds waiting when Mark, Judah Swale and Hubert Wells rode in with the prisoners and the line of horses bearing their grisly burdens. Leaving the crowd to admire the corpses, the three men man-handled the prisoners down and prodded them into the hoosegow. In the general astonishment Walt Maggs stood watching Doc Knowles minister to Ezra Cummings' wounded shoulder. Doc Knowles looked up, caught Mark's eye and smiled in an assured manner before casting a professional eye over the prisoners. 'I'll see to him next,' he said, nodding towards Denning, who was staring maliciously at Walt.

'Thanks, Doc,' Mark replied. 'He'll sure be in better hands than he deserves.'

Knowles grunted, but Mark detected plea-sure in his expression at being back inside the pale.

'What happened to him?' Mark asked of Ezra Cummings, and Walt Maggs told him.

Sharp anger rose in Mark and he had to struggle with himself to regain control, and stop himself inflicting further injury on Denning's henchman.

'It was nothing to worry about,' Doc Knowles said quickly. 'I've seen Miss Kate. She's got a lump on her head, but no compli-cations.'

Judah Swale took the prisoners through to the cells, locking up behind him, then he asked Mark to stay while he and Hubert Wells collected two more prisoners, and they left Mark congratulating young Walt Maggs for his timely intervention.

The news had reached the stage-depot, and no sooner had the door closed behind Wells than it opened again to admit Kate Lomas and Hollins. Involuntarily Kate and Mark moved towards each other, and Mark found himself holding her more tightly than medical concern required for her injury, but Kate didn't seem to mind. Knowles, now finished with Ezra Cummings, looked at them and said drily, 'I ain't gonna quarrel with you wanting a second opinion, Miss Kate, but you might have asked me.'

Kate disengaged herself unhurriedly, and as she smiled at Knowles a warm flush settled on her face. She knew, whatever else might happen, that when Doctor Holden shook the dust of Kremmling from under his feet that she would be riding right alongside him, even though it might mean living with his Indian blood-brothers as he ministered to their needs. Mark had no such conviction but he hoped he'd never lose sight of her.

Swale and Wells returned with Josiah Sloan of the Crippled Wagon and Luther Dill the store-owner in tow, and housed them in the cells with the others, and Doctor Knowles followed them in to see to Denning's wound after returning Cummings to his cell. When they all talked of eating, Walt Maggs under-took to keep guard over the prisoners and see Doc Knowles out safely, so a contented group pushed their way through appreciative townsfolk who were busy digging out the men who had taken over businesses from citizens, and running them out of town.

The farewells in town had been said. Right on time Mark was leaving for St Louis and the wagon train. White Eagle sat back, satisfied that Mark had completed all the tasks that he had promised, and glad in the knowledge that the Indian tribes had rallied behind his blood-brother when he required help, which Mark and his father had given so readily to the Indians. His tribe could now depend upon a regular supply of five hundred steers the first day after the last fall full moon, from the Lone Star and Anvil as promised by Hank Dean and Lew Tome, now returned to their ranches. The Indians were moving out of Eagle of Death Mountain, leaving the townsfolk to dig for silver if they wanted. It was enough to have a buffer of friendly whites between them and the pushy Military.

White Eagle stood up, and he and Mark embraced each other as brothers, then Mark took Chief from Crazy Hawk and climbed into the saddle. Turning the animal around in a slow circle, saluting the braves everywhere, and with a last salute to White Eagle, he took up the packhorse lead rein and rode off towards the ridge with Crazy Hawk and Walking Serpent riding either side of him. They stopped at the ridge to cheer him on, and they stayed watching until he was lost in the rolling terrain.

Mark had kept to his time schedule, and when he hit the Kremmling trail for Granby he pulled up beside the six riders who waited for him. Kate, Joe Hollins, Dale Webb, Betsy Gray, Walt Maggs and Judah Swale. Solemnly he shook hands with them, and he was surprised to find the men and Betsy grinning widely, then he noticed the saddle-roll on Kate's Palomino.

'Hubert Wells says hello and he sure hopes to meet up again sometime,' Swales said. 'He's in Granby arranging for an escort for the prisoners.'

Mark nodded. 'I sure hope to meet you all again.' Then, with a smile, he turned Chief to the right and headed for Granby.

There was a loud shout of farewell behind him, then galloping hooves caught up and Kate eased her Palomino alongside. He looked across at her, and his features melted as love for her flooded him.

'Mebbe I'll make a scout or mebbe not,' Kate said, 'but you've just got to take me. I've nowhere else to go. Pa's moving in with Hannah Lord on account he's given the stage-coach business on equal shares to Joe Hollins, Dale Webb, Walt and old Rube.

Dale and Betsy'll live above when they get married, which'll be soon.'

'Y'know, Kate. I've got me a wagon at St Louis. I mostly use any driver who wants to get to California. The chore's yours. Only thing, I mostly sleep in that wagon, so I reckon we ought to get wed. Let's stop at Granby an' do just that.'

Kate's face broke into a bright smile. 'I've been to Granby more times than I've seen longhorns, Mark; this will be the first time the thought of getting there has ever excited me.'

The publishers hope that this book has given you enjoyable reading. Large Print Books are especially designed to be as easy to see and hold as possible. If you wish a complete list of our books please ask at your local library or write directly to:

The Golden West Large Print Books
Magna House, Long Preston,
Skipton, North Yorkshire.
BD23 4ND